A Flock of Girls and Boys

Nora Perry

Contents

A FLOCK OF GIRLS
AND BOYS

BY

Nora Perry

THAT LITTLE SMITH GIRL.

CHAPTER I.

"The Pelhams are coming next month."

"Who are the Pelhams?"

Miss Agnes Brendon gave a little upward lift to her small pert nose as she exclaimed:

"Tilly Morris, you don't mean to say that you don't know who the Pelhams are?"

Tilly, thus addressed, lifted up *her* nose as she replied,--

"I do mean to say just that."

"Why, where have you lived?" was the next wondering question.

"In the wilds of New York City," answered Tilly, sarcastically.

"Where the sacred stiffies of Boston are unknown," cried Dora Robson, with a laugh.

"But the Pelhams,--I thought that everybody knew of the Pelhams at least," Agnes remarked, with a glance at Tilly that plainly expressed a doubt of her denial. Tilly caught the glance, and, still further irritated, cried impulsively,--

"Well, I never heard of them! Why should I? What have they done, pray tell, that everybody should know of them?"

"'Done'? I don't know as they've done anything. It's what they are. They are very rich and aristocratic people. Why, the Pelhams belong to one of the oldest families of Boston."

"What do I care for that?" said Tilly, tipping her head backward until it bumped against the wall of the house with a sounding bang, whereat Dora Robson gave a little giggle and exclaimed,--

"Mercy, Tilly, I heard it crack!"

Then another girl giggled,--it was another of the Robsons,--Dora's Cousin Amy; and after the giggle she said saucily,--

"Tilly's head is full of cracks already. I think we'd better call her 'Crack Brain;' we'll put it C.B., for short."

"You'd better call her L.H.,--'Level Head,'" a voice--a boy's voice--called out here.

The group of girls looked at one another in startled surprise. "Who--what!" Then Dora Robson, glancing over the piazza railing, exclaimed,--

"It's Will Wentworth. He's in the hammock! What do you mean, Willie, by hiding up like that, right under our noses, and listening to our secrets?"

"Hiding up? Well, I like that! I'd been out here for half an hour or more when you girls came to this end of the piazza."

"What in the world have you been doing for an hour in a hammock? I didn't know as you could keep still so long. Oh, you've got a book. Let me see it."

"You wouldn't care anything about it; it's a boy's book."

"Let me see it."

Will held up the book.

"Oh, 'Jack Hall'!"

"Of course, I knew you wouldn't care anything for a book that's full of boy's sports," returned Will.

"I know one girl that does," responded Dora, laughing and nodding her head.

"Who is she?" asked Will, looking incredulous.

"'T ain't me," answered Dora, more truthfully than grammatically.

"No, I guess not; and I guess you don't know any such girl."

Dora wheeled around and called, "Tilly, Tilly Morris! Come here and prove to this conceited, contradicting boy that I'm telling the truth."

"Oh, it's Tilly Morris, eh?" sung out Will.

"Yes," answered Tilly, turning and looking down at the occupant of the hammock; "I think 'Jack Hall' is the jolliest kind of a book. I've read it twice."

Will jerked himself up into a sitting posture, as he ejaculated in pleased astonishment,--

"Come, I say now!"

"Yes," went on Tilly; "I think it's one of the best books I ever read,--that part about the boat-race I've read over three or four times."

"Well, your head *is* level," cried Will, sitting up still straighter in the hammock, and regarding Tilly with a look of respect.

"Because I don't care anything for Boston's grand folks and do care for 'Jack Hall'?" laughed Tilly.

"Yes, that's about it," responded Will, with a little grin. "I'm so sick and tired," he went on, "hearing about 'swells' and money. The best fellow I know at school is quite poor; and one of the worst of the lot is what you'd call a swell, and has no end of money."

"There are all kinds of swells, Master Willie. Why, you know perfectly well that you belong to the swells yourself," retorted Dora.

"I don't!" growled Will.

"Well, I should just like to hear what your cousin Frances would say to that."

"Oh, Fan!" cried Will, contemptuously.

"If you don't think much of the old Wentworth name--"

"I do think much of it," interrupted Will. "I think so much of it that I want to live up to it. The old Wentworths were splendid fellows, some of 'em; and all of 'em were jolly and generous and independent. There wasn't any sneaking little brag and snobbishness in 'em. They 'd have cut a fellow dead that had come around with that sort of stuff;" and sixteen-year-old Will nodded his head with an emphatic movement that showed his approval of this trait in his ancestors.

Dora looked at him curiously; then with a faint smile she said,--

"Your cousin Frances is so proud of those old Wentworths. She's often told me how grandly they lived, and she's so pleased that her name Frances is the name of one of the prettiest of the Governor's wives."

"Yes; and one of the prettiest, and I dare say one of the best of 'em, was a servant-girl in Governor Benning Wentworth's kitchen, and he married her out of it. Did Fan ever tell you that?" and Will chuckled.

Amy Robson stared at Will with amazement as she exclaimed,--

"Well, I never saw such a queer boy as you are,--to run your own family down."

"I'm not running 'em down. 'Tisn't running 'em down to say that one of 'em married Martha Hilton. Martha Hilton was a nice girl, though she was poor and had to work in a kitchen. Plenty of nice girls--farmers' daughters--worked in that way in those old times; the New England histories tell you that."

Not one of the girls made any comment or criticism upon this statement, for Will Wentworth was known to be well up in history; but after a moment or two of silence, Dora burst forth in this wise,--

"You may talk as you like. Will Wentworth, but you know perfectly well that you don't think a servant-girl is as good as you are."

"If you mean that I don't think she is of the same class, of course I don't. She may be a great deal better than I am in other ways, for all that. In those old days, though, the servant-girls weren't the kind we have now; they were Americans,-- farmers' daughters,--most of 'em."

"Oh, well, you may talk and talk in this grand way, Willie Wentworth; but you know where you belong, and when the Pelhams come, Tilly'll see for herself that you are one of the same sort."

"As the Pelhams?"

"Well, what have you got to say about the Pelhams in that scornful way?" asked Amy, rather indignantly.

"I'm not scornful. I was only going to set you right, and say that the Pelhams are fashionable folks and the Wentworths are not."

"Oh, I'd like to have your cousin Fanny hear you say that. Fanny thinks the Wentworths are fully equal to the Pelhams or any one else."

"They are."

"What do you mean, Will Wentworth? You just said--"

"I just said that the Pelhams were fashionable people and the Wentworths were not, but that doesn't make the Pelhams any better than the Wentworths. The Pelhams have got more money and like to spend it in that way,--in being fashion- able society folks, I suppose. There are lots of people who have as much and more money, who won't be fashionable,--they don't like it."

"Your cousin Fanny says--"

"Fanny's a snob. It makes me sick to hear her talk sometimes. If she were here now, she'd be full of these Pelhams, and as thick with 'em when they came, whether they were nice or not. If they were ever so nice, she'd snub 'em if they were not up in the world,--what you call 'swells.' She never got such stuff as that from the Wentworths."

"There are plenty of people like your cousin," spoke up Tilly, with sudden emphasis and a fleeting glance at Agnes Brendon.

"Oh, now, Tilly, don't say that," cried Dora, in a funny little wheedling tone, "don't now; you'll hurt some of our feelings, for we shall think you mean one of us, and you can't mean that, Tilly dear,"--the wheedling tone taking on a droll, merry accent,--"you can't, for you know how independent and high-minded we all are,-- how incapable of such meanness!"

"I wouldn't trust this high-mindedness," retorted Tilly, wrinkling up her forehead.

"Now, Tilly, you don't mean that,--you don't mean that you've come all the way from naughty New York to find such dreadful faults in nice, primmy New England. The very dogs here are above such things. Look at Punch there making friends with that little plebeian yellow dog."

"And look at Dandy barking at everybody who isn't well dressed," laughed Tilly, pointing to a handsome collie, who was vigorously giving voice to his displeasure at the approach of a workman in shabby clothing.

The Robson girls and Will Wentworth joined in Tilly's laugh; but Agnes Brendon, who could never see a joke, looked disgusted, and glancing at the little yellow dog, asked petulantly,--

"Whose dog is it?"

"It belongs to the girl who sits at the corner table," answered Will Wentworth, "and its name is Pete. I heard the girl call him this morning."

"What a horrid, vulgar name!" exclaimed Agnes. "It suits the dog, though; and the people, I suppose, are--"

"Oh, Agnes, look at that horrid worm on your dress!"

Agnes jumped up in a panic, screaming, "Where, where?"

Dora, bending down to brush off the smallest of small caterpillars, whispered,--

"The girl who owns the yellow dog is in the other hammock. I just saw her, and she can hear every word you say."

"I don't care if she does hear," said Agnes, without troubling herself to lower her voice. "You needn't have frightened me with your horrid worm story, just for that."

Will Wentworth, as he heard this, fell backward into his reclining position, with an explosive laugh. The next minute he sprang out of the hammock, and, tucking "Jack Hall" under his arm, was up and off, giving a sidelong look as he went at the other hammock, which, though only a few rods away, was half hidden by the foliage of the two low-growing trees between which it hung. Meeting Tilly and the Robson girls as he ran around the corner of the house, he said breathlessly,--

"Look here; that girl must have heard everything that we've said."

"Well, there wasn't anything said that concerned her, until Agnes began about the yellow dog; and I stopped that," said Dora, gleefully.

"She may be acquainted with the Pelhams,--how do we know?" exclaimed Will, ruefully.

"The Pelhams!" cried Dora and Amy, in one breath.

"Yes, how do we know?" repeated Will.

"That girl who sits over at the corner table with that stuffy old woman, acquainted with the Pelhams! Oh, Will, if Agnes could hear you!" cried Dora, with a shout of laughter.

"Well, I can't see what there is to laugh at," broke in Will, huffily. "Why shouldn't she and the stuffy old woman, as you call her, know the Pelhams? She's a nice-looking girl, a first-rate looking girl. What's the matter with her?"

"Matter? I don't know that anything is the matter, except that she doesn't look like the sort of girl who would be an acquaintance of the Pelhams. She doesn't look like their kind, you know. She wears the plainest sort of dresses,--just little straight up and down frocks of brown or drab, or those white cambric things,--they are more like baby-slips than anything; and her hats are just the same,--great flat all-round hats, not a bit of style to them; and she's a girl of fourteen or fifteen certainly. Do you suppose people of the Pelhams' kind dress like that?"

Will gave a gruff little sound half under his breath, as he asked sarcastically,--

"How do people of the Pelham kind dress?"

"Oh, like Dora and Amy, and especially like Agnes,--in the height of the fashion, you know," Tilly cried laughingly.

"Now, Tilly," expostulated Dora, "neither Amy nor I overdress. We wear what all girls of our age--girls who are almost young ladies--wear, and I'm sure you wear the same kind of things."

"Not quite, Dora. I'll own, though, I would if I could; but there's such a lot of us at home that the money gives out before it goes all 'round," said Tilly, frankly, yet rather ruefully.

"I'm sure you look very nice," said Dora, politely. Amy echoed the polite remark, while Will, eying the three with an attempt at a critical estimate, thought to himself, "They don't look a bit nicer than that girl at the corner table."

But Will was too wise to give utterance to this thought. He knew how it would be received; he knew that the three would laugh at him and say, "What does a boy know about girl's clothes?"

In the mean time, while all this was going on, what was that girl who had suggested the talk, that girl who sat at the corner table in the dining room and who was now lying in a hammock,--what was she doing, what was she thinking?

CHAPTER II.

She was lying looking up through the green branches of the trees. She had been reading, but her book was now closed, and she was lying quietly looking up at the blue sky between the branches. Her thoughts were not quite so quiet as her position would seem to indicate. She had, as Will Wentworth had said, heard all that talk about the Pelhams. Whatever her class in life, she was certainly a delicate and honorable young girl; for at the very first, when she found that it was a talk between a party of friends, and they were unconscious of a stranger's near neighborhood, she had done her best to make her presence known to them by various little coughs and ahems, and once or twice by decided movements, and readjustments of her position. As no attention was paid to these demonstrations, she finally concluded that none of the party cared whether they were overheard or not, and so settled herself comfortably back again into her place, and opened her book.

But she could not read much. These talkers were all about her own age, and if they did not care that a stranger was overhearing what they said, she need not trouble herself any more; and it was quite certain she found the talk amusing, for more than once a ripple of merriment would dimple her face, and the laughter would nearly break forth from her lips. Even at the last, when Agnes spoke so scornfully of the little yellow dog, the girl seemed to be more amused than annoyed; and she quite understood Miss Agnes's unfinished sentence, too, and Dora's little device to make it unfinished.

It was then only that she saw that her attempts to inform the party of her near neighborhood had been unsuccessful. She got rather red as this knowledge was forced upon her; then, like Will Wentworth, she burrowed down deeper than ever in the hammock, and gave way to a little burst of laughter, though, unlike Will's, hers was no noisy explosion.

All the time she was watching Will and the girls as they took their way across the lawn; and as soon as they disappeared from her view, she jumped from the hammock, and with the fleetest of fleet footsteps ran into the house. Coming down the long wide hall, she met the very person she was going in search of,--the person that Dora Robson had called "that stuffy old woman;" and trotting after her was the little yellow dog, who had just been washed and brushed until his short hair shone like satin.

"Oh, Pete, Pete, come here!" and Pete at this invitation flew to his young mistress's arms with much demonstration of delight.

"And they called you a vulgar plebeian dog, Pete, just think of that!" cried the girl, as she fondled the little animal.

"Who called him that, Peggy?" asked her companion, in a surprised tone.

"One of those girls at the table by the window. Oh, auntie, I want to tell you about it. I was coming to find you on purpose to tell you. Let's go in here, where we shall be all by ourselves," turning towards a small unoccupied reception-room.

There, cosily ensconced beside her aunt, with the little yellow dog at her feet, the dog's mistress told her story, with various exclamations and interjections of, "Now wasn't it horrid of them?" and "Did you ever know anything so ridiculous?" while auntie listened with great interest, her only comment at the end being,--

"Well, they're not worth minding, Peggy, and I wouldn't act as if I'd heard what they said when you meet them. I wouldn't take any notice of them."

"I? Why, it's they who won't take any notice of me, auntie. I'm like my little dog,--a vulgar plebeian. What would they say, what would they think, if they could hear you call me Peggy?--that's as bad as Pete, isn't it?"

"I'm afraid it is;" and auntie laughed a little as she spoke.

The great summer hotel was not nearly full yet, for it was only the last of June; and as Peggy went down to luncheon, her hand closely clasped in "auntie's," whom should she meet face to face in the rather deserted-looking hall but "those girls"? It was a little embarrassing all round, and they all colored up very rosily as they met.

"I wonder where the boy is?" thought Peggy; "he and that New York girl were nice." She glanced over her shoulder at this thought. There was the boy; and--yes, he was standing at the office desk, carefully examining the hotel register. "He's looking for our names!" flashed into Peggy's mind, "and those girls set him up to it. I wonder what they'll say to 'Mrs. Smith and niece'? I know; they'll say, or the girl they call Agnes will say, 'Smith, of course! I knew they had some such common name as that.'"

Something very like this comment did take place when Master Will, in obedience to Dora Robson's request, brought the information that the people at the corner table were Mrs. Smith and her niece. But if Peggy could only have heard Will flash out upon this comment the further information that very distinguished people had borne the name of Smith,--could have heard him quote the famous English clergyman Sydney Smith, whose wit and humor were so charming,--if Peggy could have heard Will going on in this fashion, she would have thought he was very nice indeed, and been quite delighted with his independent outspokenness.

Agnes, however, was anything but delighted. She was, in fact, very angry with Will by this time, and what she called his meddlesome, domineering airs, and quite determined to let him know at the very first opportunity that she was not in the least to be influenced by his opinions.

The opportunity presented itself sooner than she expected. It was just after luncheon, and a couple of Indians had come up from their neighboring summer camp with a load of baskets for sale.

Dora and Tilly, with Mrs. Brendon and Agnes and Amy, went out to them at once. Others soon followed, and a brisk bargaining began. When the Indian woman held up a beautiful little basket skilfully woven to imitate shells, there was a general exclamation of pleasure, and one voice cried out with enthusiasm, "Oh, how lovely!" and the owner of the voice reached forth to take the basket in her hand. Agnes Brendon, turning quickly, saw that it was Mrs. Smith's niece.

"The idea of that girl pushing herself forward like this!" was Agnes's whispered remark to Amy.

"Hush: she'll hear you," whispered back Amy.

"I don't care," answered Agnes, at the same time crowding herself to the front and inquiring the price of the basket, with the determination to get possession of it before any one else had a chance. But when the price--two dollars--was named, Mrs. Brendon pronounced it exorbitant, and offered half the sum, never doubting its acceptance. The Indian woman, however, shook her head with an air of grim decision; and at that very moment, catching sight of Mrs. Smith and her niece, she nodded smilingly, repeated the price, and held the basket up again;

"Yes, yes, I'll take it," called out Peggy, nodding and smiling responsively; and the next instant the basket was in her hands.

Agnes, not only disappointed, but deeply mortified and angry, turned hastily to Dora Robson, and gave vent to her feelings by remarking in a perfectly clear undertone,--

"The worst of a place like this is that you meet such common people, with nothing to recommend them but their money."

Dora and Amy flushed with annoyance at this speech; but Tilly was so disgusted and indignant that she broke away from them all with an impatient exclamation, and started off across the lawn towards the house. Halfway across she met Will Wentworth, with Tom Raymond,--a great chum of his, who had just arrived by the noon boat.

"Hullo, what's up, what's the matter?" asked Will, as he perceived the expression of Tilly's face.

Tilly stopped, and in a few graphic words told her story, winding up with, "Wasn't it horrid of Agnes?"

"Horrid? It was beastly," sputtered Will. "*She* to call people common!"

"But that girl is not common," said Tilly. "She may belong to people who have just made a lot of money,--for that's what Agnes meant to fling out,--but there isn't any vulgar common show of it. Look at her, how plainly she's dressed, and how quiet she is."

"Wonder what Agnes is up to now? Let's go and see," said Will, wheeling about and nodding to Tilly and Tom to follow.

As they came along together, Will a little ahead, Tom Raymond was quite silent until they approached the group collected around the Indians; then he suddenly ejaculated, "Well, I never!"

"What? What do you mean?--what--who do you see?" asked Tilly, very much surprised at this outbreak.

"Is that the girl--the Smith girl you were telling about--there by the tree--holding a basket?" asked Tom.

"Yes; why--do you know her?"

"N-o--but--I was thinking--she doesn't look common, does she?"

"Of course she doesn't, only plainly dressed."

"Yes, that's all;" and Tom gave a little odd chuckling laugh.

"How queer Tom Raymond is!" thought Tilly. She thought he was queerer still, as she caught his furtive glances toward that Smith girl. Presently Miss Tilly saw that the Smith girl was regarding Tom with rather a puzzled observation.

"I see how it is," reflected Miss Tilly; "they have met before somewhere, and Tom doesn't want to know her now. He thinks she isn't fine enough for this Boston set, though he owns that she doesn't look common. Oh, I do believe that Will Wentworth is the only one here who has any sense or heart."

As Tilly arrived at this conclusion of her reflections, Will came running up to her.

"Come," he said, "there's no fun here. Let's go and have a game of tennis."

"But where's Agnes? I thought you wanted to see what she was doing."

"She's gone off in a huff because I asked her if she'd bought any baskets," answered Will, grinning. Tilly laughed, and Tom Raymond gave another odd little chuckle. Then the three strolled away to the tennis ground. As they were passing the rustic bench under the tree where Mrs. Smith and her niece were sitting, Tilly took a sudden resolution, and, stopping abruptly, said,--

"We're going to have a game of tennis; won't you join us, Miss--Miss Smith?"

The girl looked up with a smile, hesitated a moment, and then accepted the invitation. Will, nodding to Tilly a surprised and pleased approval of her action, started off ahead of the others to see if the tennis ground was occupied. As he turned the corner, he met Dora Robson with a racket in her hand.

"Oh," she cried, "here you are! I was just coming after you, for Amy and I have got to go in,--mamma has sent for us, and Agnes was so disappointed,--now it's all right, for there's Tilly, and--what luck--Tom Raymond; he's such a splendid player, and you can--" But Dora stopped, open-mouthed and wide-eyed. Who--who was that behind Tilly?

CHAPTER III.

As Agnes, standing waiting upon the tennis-ground where Dora had left her, suddenly caught sight of Tom Raymond, her heart gave a little throb of exultation. Tom Raymond was the best tennis-player she knew. To have him for her partner would be delightful, and she went forward with the most gracious welcome to him. So absorbed was she, so pleased at Tom's appearance, at his polite response to her, she did not observe Miss Smith,--did not see Tilly draw back, did not hear her say, "No, I don't care to play, Miss Smith, I want you to play with Will; this is my friend Will Wentworth, Miss Smith," by way of introduction.

No; Agnes saw and heard nothing of all this, or of Will's polite arrangements with the newcomer. She saw nothing, she thought of nothing, but that her own little arrangement to have Tom for a partner was successful; and so, blithely and triumphantly, she took her place and lifted her racket. Whizz! she sent the ball flying over the netting, and whizz! it came flying back again, to be returned by Tom Raymond's vigorous stroke. Agnes regarded this stroke with due admiration. "Neither Will nor Tilly can match that," she thought; and at the thought she looked over and across the netting, to see a girl's uplifted arm swinging easily forward, the racket hitting the ball lightly with a swift, sure, upward, and onward motion. Where had Tilly learned to strike out like that, all at once? Tilly! The uplifted arm that had partially hidden the player's face was lowered. What--what--it was not Tilly, but--but--that girl! How did she come there? A glance at Will's face drawn up into a most exasperating grin, at Will's eyes darting forth gleams of fun, was enough for Agnes.

Yes, this was Will Wentworth's doing,--this hateful plot to humiliate her and triumph over her. Stung by this thought, she lost sight for that moment of every-thing else, and the ball sent so surely back to her dropped to the ground before her partner could rescue it. An exclamation of disappointment from Tom added to her discomfiture; and when Will, the next instant, cried, "Wait a minute, till I get another racket, Miss Smith has broken hers," Agnes, flinging down her own, exclaimed,--

"Miss Smith can have my racket; I'm not going to play any longer!"

"Not going to play? What do you mean?" shouted Will.

"I mean that I am not used to a surprise-party and to playing with strangers," was the rude and angry answer.

"You--you ought to--" But Will controlled himself and stopped. He was about to say, "You ought to be ashamed of yourself."

Agnes, however, understood by the tone of his voice something of what he meant, and turned scornfully away, her head up, and with a glance at Tom that plainly showed she expected him to follow her.

But Tom made no movement of that kind. He stood where he was, looking across at Will, who, red and ashamed, had approached Miss Smith, and was evi-dently making some sort of apology to her for the insult that had been offered to her; and Miss Smith was listening to this apology with the coolest little face imagin-able.

Tom, taking all this in, gave another of his odd little chuckles. Agnes heard it, and flushed scarlet. So he was taking sides with Will Wentworth, was he? And what--what--was that--Tilly? Yes, it was Tilly,--Tilly with the racket she, Agnes, had flung down,--Tilly standing in her place and--and--serving the ball back to that girl! So Tilly was with them too? Well, she would see, they would all see, that Agnes Brendon was not a person to be snubbed and disregarded in this fashion, nor a person to be forced to make acquaintances with vulgar or common people against her will. Oh, they would see, they would see! And bracing herself up with these indignant resolutions, Agnes betook herself to the hotel.

Before the end of the week there were two distinct parties in the house, where heretofore there had been but one,--two distinct opposing forces.

On one side were Agnes and Dora and Amy; on the other side were Tilly and Tom and Will. Dora and Amy were not naturally ill-natured girls, but they were inclined to be worldly and were greatly under Agnes's influence. She had been a sort of authority with them for a good while, perforce of her dominant disposition and the knowledge she seemed to possess of the worldly matters that were of so much interest to them.

"But I should think you would feel ashamed to side with Agnes Brendon in persecuting a poor little stranger," said honest Tilly, a day or two after the tennis affair; for Agnes had at once set to work to carry out her plan of showing that she was not to be forced, as she expressed it, into making acquaintances she didn't like, and had thus lost no opportunity of being disagreeable.

Dora flushed at Tilly's words, but she answered coolly,--

"Persecuting! I don't call it persecuting to avoid a person one doesn't want to know."

"Yes; but how does Agnes avoid her? She stiffens herself up and curls her lips when the girl goes by, as if there was something contaminating about her; and one night when we were in the music-room and Miss Smith was playing and singing 'Mrs. Brady' for us, Agnes came in with Amy and made a great fuss and noise, disturbing everybody in pretending to hunt up one of her own music-books; and when I asked her to be quieter, she said something horrid about 'low common songs,' and 'Mrs. Brady' isn't a low common song; and the other morning, when Pete, the little dog, ran up to her on the piazza, she pushed him away from her in such a disagreeable manner--and so it has gone on every day, and I think it's a shame, and such a nice girl as Miss Smith is too. I told grandmother all about it,--the whole story,--and she says it is Agnes who is vulgar and not Miss Smith, and that she never would have brought me here if she had known that a girl who could behave like that was to be in the house; and you can tell Miss Agnes Brendon this, if you like, and you can tell her too that she'll only make us stand by Miss Smith stancher than ever by persecuting her as she does."

"I shall tell her nothing of the kind, and there's no such thing as persecution anyway,--that's ridiculous. Agnes is very exclusive,--the Brendons all are,--and she doesn't like to make acquaintances with common people, that's all."

"Common people! Miss Smith isn't any more common than you or I. She's a very ladylike girl.--much more ladylike and nice, and nicer-looking too, than Agnes."

"Nicer looking with those plain frocky dresses, and her hair all pulled back without the sign of a crimp or curl!" and Dora burst into a jeering laugh.

"Oh, she isn't all fussed up, I know, as most of us girls are; but her clothes are of the very finest materials,--I've noticed that."

"And that stuffy old aunt's clothes are of the finest material, I suppose; and the little yellow dog's coat is as fine as a King Charles spaniel's," jeered Dora.

"Stuffy old aunt! She isn't stuffy in the least. She's a little old-fashioned; that's all. Grandmother has taken quite a fancy to her."

Dora smiled a very provoking smile as she said,--

"Perhaps the Pelhams, when they come, will take a fancy to her too, and to that pretty name of Peggy."

The hot color rushed to Tilly's cheeks and the tears to her eyes as she turned away. She knew perfectly well that Dora was thinking: "Oh, your grandmother is only another old woman a good deal like Mrs. Smith,--what is her judgment worth?"

Dora was a little ashamed of herself as Tilly left her. Indeed, she had been a little ashamed of herself for some time,--ever since, in fact, she had ranged herself on Agnes's side after the tennis affair; but once having taken that side she was determined to stick to it, and to believe that it was the right side, in spite of some qualms of conscience.

Her cousin Amy followed in the same path, and Agnes spared no pains to keep them there. She felt that she could not afford to lose her only allies. Every minute that had elapsed since she had flung down her tennis racket in such anger and mortification had but increased this mortification, and strengthened her resolve to show those boys and Tilly Morris that she was right and they were wrong about "that girl."

Of course, when she set her face in this direction, she was on the lookout for everything unfavorable; and everything, pretty nearly, was turned into something unfavorable, so perverted and distorted had her vision become. It was "Dora, did you notice this?" and "Amy, did you see that?" until the two began to find the incessant harping upon one subject rather wearisome, especially as the particular details thus pointed out had never yet developed into matters of any importance.

"I wish Agnes wouldn't keep talking about that Smith girl all the time, unless there was something more worth while to talk about," broke forth Dora impatiently to Amy just after the interview with Tilly.

"So do I," Amy responded emphatically; then, laughing a little, "unless there was some real big thing to tell."

"But I don't wonder Agnes doesn't like the girl, with Tilly and Will taking up for her and making such a fuss;" and Dora indignantly repeated Tilly's accusations. Amy caught at the word "persecution," as Dora had done, and together they defended themselves against these accusations with a zeal and ingenuity worthy of a better cause.

They were in the full tide of this talk when, as they rounded the curve of the shore where they were walking, they came upon Agnes herself, coming rapidly towards them.

"Oh, girls, I've been looking for you everywhere. I've got something I want to show you," she exclaimed excitedly. "Come up here and sit down;" and she led the way to a little cluster of rocks.

Dora and Amy glanced at each other rather apprehensively. Was Agnes going to tell them something else about the Smith girl,--going to say. "Did you notice this?" or "Did you see that?" in reference to some detail that displeased her? They had worked themselves up into quite a state of indignation against Tilly and the boys, and of increased sympathy with Agnes; but they were so tired of hearing, "Did you notice this?" "Did you see that?" when there had been such uninteresting little things to "notice," to "see."

With these apprehensions flitting through their minds, the two girls seated themselves to listen with very languid interest. But what was that Agnes was unfolding,--a newspaper? And what was it she was saying as she pointed to a certain column? She wanted them to read that! The cousins looked at each other in a dazed, inquiring fashion; and Agnes, starting forward, impatiently thrust the paper into Dora's hand and cried sharply,--

"Read that; read that!"

Dora in a bewildered way read aloud this sentence, which in big black letters stared her in the face,--

"Smithson, alias Smith."

"Well, go on, go on; read what is underneath," urged Agnes, as Dora stopped;

and Dora went on and read,--

"It seems that that arch schemer and swindler Frank Smithson, who got him-self out of the country so successfully with his ill-gotten gains from the Star Mining Company, has dropped the last syllable from his too notorious name, and is now fig-uring in South America under the name of Smith. His wife and young son are with him, and the three are living luxuriously in the suburbs of Rio, where Smithson has rented a villa. An older child, a daughter of fourteen or fifteen, was left behind in this country with Smithson's brother's widow, who has also taken the name of Smith. They are staying at a summer resort not far from Boston."

The bewildered look on Dora's face did not disappear as she came to the end of this statement.

"What did you want me to read this for?" she asked Agnes.

"What did I want you to read it for? Is it possible that you don't see,--that you don't understand?"

"Understand what? We don't know these Smithsons."

"But we do know these--Smiths."

"Agnes, you don't mean--"

"Yes, I do mean that I believe--that I am sure that these Smiths are those very identical Smithsons."

"Oh, Agnes, what makes you think so? Smith is such a very common name, you know."

"Yes, I know it; but here is a girl whose name is Smith, and she is with a Mrs. Smith, her aunt, and they are staying at a summer resort near Boston. How does that fit?"

"Oh, Agnes, it does look like--as if it must be, doesn't it?" cried Dora, in a sort of shuddering enjoyment of the sensational situation.

"Of course it does. I knew I was right about those people. I knew there was something queer and mysterious about them. And what do you think,--only yes-terday I happened to go into the little parlor, where there are writing-materials, and there sat this very Peggy Smith directing a letter; and when she went out, I happened to cast my eyes at the blotting-pad she had used, and I couldn't help reading--for it was just as plain as print--the last part of the address, and it was--'South America'!"

CHAPTER IV.

"I don't believe it! I don't believe it!" said Tilly Morris, indignantly, as Dora wound up her recital of the Smithson-Smith story.

"Well, you can believe it or not; but I don't see how you can help believing, when you remember that their name is Smith, and that they are aunt and niece, and that the niece is fourteen or fifteen,--just as the paper said,--and that they are staying at a summer resort not far from Boston, and--that the niece writes to some one in South America,--think of that!"

Tilly thought, and, flushing scarlet as she thought, she burst out,--

"Well, I don't care, I don't care. I'm not going to talk about it, either. How many people have you--has Amy--has Agnes told?"

"I haven't told anybody but you yet. I've just come from Agnes."

"Yet! Now, look here, let me tell you something, Dora. My father, you know, is a lawyer, and I've heard him talk a great deal when we've had company at dinner about queer things that people did and said,--queer things, I mean, that got them into lawsuits. One of the things that I particularly remember was a case where a woman told things that she had heard and things that she had fancied against a neighbor, and the neighbor went to law about it, prosecuted the woman for slander, and they had a horrid time. The woman's daughters had to go into court and be examined as witnesses. Oh, it was horrid; and the worst of it was that even though there was some truth in the stories, there were things that were not true,--exaggerations, you know,--and so the woman was declared guilty, and her husband had to pay a lot of money to keep her out of prison. There was ever so much more that I've forgotten; but I recollect papa's turning to us children at the end, and saying, 'Now, children, remember when you are repeating things that you have heard against people, that the next thing you'll know you may be prosecuted for what you've said, and have to answer for it in the law courts.'"

Dora looked scared. "Well, I'm sure," she began, "I haven't repeated this to anybody but you; and if Agnes--"

"What's that about me?" suddenly interrupted Agnes herself, as she came up behind the two girls. Dora began to explain, and then called upon Tilly to repeat her story of the lawsuit.

"Oh, fiddlesticks!" cried Agnes, angrily, after hearing this story; "you can't frighten me that way, Tilly Morris. We can't be prosecuted for telling facts that are already in the newspapers."

"But we can be for what isn't. It isn't in the newspapers that this Mrs. Smith and her niece are these Smithsons."

"Well, Tilly Morris, I should think it was in the newspapers about as plain as could be. What do you say to this sentence?" And Agnes pulled from her pocket the Smithson article she had cut out, and read aloud: "'An older child--a daughter of fourteen or fifteen--was left behind in this country with Smithson's brother's widow, who has also taken the name of Smith. They are staying at a summer resort not far from Boston;' and what do you say to that letter addressed to some place in South America?"

"I say that--that--all this might mean somebody else, and not--not these--our--my Smiths. What did your mother say when you told her, and showed the paper to her?"

"I didn't tell her; I didn't show her the paper. We never tell mamma such things; she is a nervous invalid, and it would fret her to death," Agnes responded snappishly.

"Well, I don't believe it's my Smiths; I believe it's somebody else," flashed back Tilly, with tears in her eyes and in her voice.

"Oh, very well; you can stand up for your Smiths, if you like; but you'll find they are--"

"Hullo! What's the little Smith girl done now? Agnes, I should think you'd get tired of rattling about the Smiths," interposed a voice here.

It was Will Wentworth's voice; he had come out on the piazza just as the girls were passing the hall door.

Agnes started back nervously at the sight of him. "I think you are very rude to listen and spring at anybody like this," she said.

Will looked at her in astonishment. "I haven't been listening, and I didn't spring at you," he responded indignantly. "I simply met you as I came out, and heard you say something about the Smiths."

"What did you hear?" asked Agnes, quickly.

"I heard you say to Tilly, 'Stand up for your Smiths if you like;' and I knew by that you'd been going for Miss Peggy, and Tilly had been defending her." Will's bright eyes, as he said this, suddenly observed that there was something unusually serious in the girl's face. "What's the matter?" he inquired; "what's up now?"

Agnes put her hand into her pocket, and Tilly drew in her breath with a little gasp, and braced herself to come to the defence again when Agnes should answer this question, as she fully expected her to do, by producing the cutting from the newspaper and repeating her accusations. But when Agnes drew her hand forth, there was no slip of paper in it, and all the answer that she made to Will's question was to say in a mocking tone,--

"Ask Tilly; she knows all the delightful facts now about Miss Peggy and her highly respectable family."

The decisive tone in which this was said, the significant expression of the speaker's face as she glanced at Tilly, and Tilly's own silence at the moment impressed Will very strongly, as Agnes fully intended; and when a minute later she slipped her hand over Dora's arm, and went off with her toward the tennis ground, and Tilly refused to tell him what this something that was "up" was, honest Will felt convinced that the "something" must be very queer indeed.

Poor Tilly saw and understood at once the nature of the impression that Will had received; but what could she do? It was certainly better to keep silence than to speak and tell that dreadful, dreadful story of "Smithson, alias Smith." Even, yes, even if it was true,--for Tilly, spite of her vehement defence, her stout declaration of disbelief at the first, had a shuddering fear at her heart as she thought of that last paragraph about the girl of fourteen or fifteen, and of that letter to South America,--a shuddering fear that the story might be true; but even then she would not be one of those to point a finger at poor innocent Peggy; for, whatever her father might have done, Peggy was innocent.

There was one person, however, that Tilly could speak to, could ask counsel of, and that, of course, was her grandmother. Grandmother, she was quite sure, would agree with her that the story was not to be chattered about; and even if it were true that Mrs. Smith and Peggy were those very Smithsons, neither was to blame, but only, as she had heard her father say once of the family of a man who had proved a defaulter, "innocent victims who were very much to be pitied."

But perhaps--perhaps grandmother would not believe that Mrs. Smith and Peggy were "those Smithsons," and perhaps she would find some careful way to investigate the matter and prove that they were not. With this hope springing up over her fears, Tilly flew along the corridor to her grandmother's room.

"What! what! what!" cried grandmother, as she listened to the story; "I don't believe a word of Agnes's suspicions. There are millions of Smiths in the world."

"But did you hear what I said about that last paragraph,--the girl of fourteen or fifteen, and--and the letter,--the letter to South America?" asked Tilly, tremulously.

"In what paper was it that Agnes found the statement?"

"It was some morning paper: I don't know which one,--I only remember seeing the date."

Grandmother rang the bell, and sent for all the morning papers. When they were brought her, she put on her spectacles and began the search for "Smithson, alias Smith." One, two, three papers she searched through; and at last there it was,--"Smithson, alias Smith!"

Tilly watched her grandmother as she read with breathless anxiety, and her heart sank as she noticed how serious was the expression on the reader's face as she came to the last paragraph.

"Oh, grandmother," she cried, "you do believe it may be our Smiths."

"Well, yes, my dear, I believe that it may possibly be, that's all; but it may not be, just as possibly."

"Oh, grandmother, couldn't you inquire--carefully, you know."

"No, no, my dear. If it isn't our Smiths, think what an outrage any inquiries would be; and if it is, how cruel to stir the matter up! No, we must say nothing. The girl is an innocent creature; and if this Smithson is her father, I doubt if she has been told by anybody the facts of the case,--probably there was some very different reason given her for dropping that last syllable of the name. However it may be, it would be cruel for us to show by our manner or speech any knowledge of the story; for either way, whether they are those Smithsons or not, Agnes has made a very unpleasant situation for them, and we must be good to them."

"But, grandmother, when Agnes tells other people--"

"She won't. Your little warning, by your description of the way she took it, convinces me that she won't."

"But other people read the papers, and they--"

"May not take any more notice than I did, if Agnes's spiteful suspicions are held in check."

"But if poor Peggy herself--"

"Peggy probably doesn't read the newspapers any more than you do. But we needn't waste time in thinking what if this or that; the clear duty for us is to take no notice, and, as I said, be good to them."

"Oh, grandmother, you are such a dear! I knew you'd feel like this."

There was to be an early little dance that night for the young people, and Tilly put on her prettiest gown,--a white mull with rose-colored ribbons,--and went down to dinner in it, for the dance was an informal affair that was to follow very soon after dinner on account of the youth of most of the dancers. Her heart beat more quickly as she looked across at the corner table and saw Peggy and her aunt in their places, and that Peggy was also dressed for the occasion in something white, embroidered with rosebuds, and with ribbon loops of pale blue and a broad sash of the same color.

"Of course, she expects to dance," thought Tilly, "and Agnes will be horrid to her about it in some way or other; but I shall stand by Peggy anyway, whatever anybody else may do."

It was with this kind intention that Tilly hurried through her dinner and has-tened out to join Peggy and her aunt when they left the dining-room. But the kind intention was arrested for the moment by Dora's voice calling out,--

"Tilly, Tilly, wait a minute."

The next thing Dora had her hand over Tilly's arm. Amy and Agnes were just behind, and there was nothing to do but to follow the general movement with them to the piazza. That it was a planned movement to separate her from Peggy, Tilly did not doubt; for once out on the piazza, Agnes, with a whispered word to Amy, turned sharply about in the opposite direction to that where Mrs. Smith and her niece were sitting.

A color like a red rose sprang to Tilly's cheeks as she glanced across at Peggy, and bowed to her with a swift little smile. Then, "How pretty Peggy Smith looks!"

and "What a lovely gown she has on!" she said, turning a brave and half-defiant glance upon Agnes.

"Yes, it is pretty. It's made of that South American embroidered muslin,--convent work, you know," answered Agnes, casting a fleeting look at Tilly.

"No, I didn't know," answered Tilly, trying to seem calm and indifferent, but failing miserably.

"Yes," went on Agnes, "I know, because my cousins have had several of those dresses, and I'm quite familiar with them."

Peggy, sitting there in her odd pretty dress, saw with pity the distress in her friend Tilly's face.

"Those girls are worrying poor Tilly, auntie, see,--and I dare say it's on my account, for I was sure when she came out that she was intending to join us, and that they prevented her,--and, auntie, I'm going to brave the lions in their dens, and going over to her."

"They are ill-bred girls, and they may do or say something rude," replied auntie, regarding Peggy with a slightly anxious expression.

"Oh, I don't care for that now. Tilly is such a darling in sticking to me, in spite of their disapproval," laughing a little, "that I think I ought to stick to her;" and, nodding to her auntie, Peggy started on her friendly errand.

"What impudence! She's actually coming over to us uninvited. Well, I must say she has nerve!" muttered Agnes, as she observed Peggy's movements.

Coming forward, Peggy nodded to the whole group of girls; but it was to Tilly she addressed herself, and by Tilly's side she seated herself. It was in doing this that the delicate material of her dress caught in a protruding nail in the splint piazza chair with an ominous sound.

"Oh, your pretty gown! it's torn!" cried Tilly.

The two sprang up to examine it, and found an ugly little rent that had nearly pulled out one of the wrought rosebuds.

"It's too bad,--too bad!" sympathized Tilly.

"But it's easily mended, and it won't show," answered Peggy, cheerfully.

"It isn't easy to mend that South American stuff so that it won't show," remarked Agnes, coolly.

"I know it isn't usually," answered Peggy, as coolly; "but auntie can mend almost anything."

"It is a perfectly beautiful dress. I wish I had one just like it," broke forth Tilly, hurriedly, hardly knowing what she was saying in the desire to say something kind.

"You could easily send for one like it," spoke up Agnes, "if you knew anybody out there, or what shop or convent address to send to."

"We could send for you," said Peggy, turning to Tilly. Tilly looked startled.

"Have you friends out there?" asked Agnes, with an impertinent stare at Peggy.

"Yes," answered Peggy, curtly, meeting Agnes's stare with a look of sudden haughtiness.

Tilly turned hot and cold, but through all her perturbation was one feeling of satisfaction. Peggy could stand her ground, it seemed, and resent impertinence; but, "Oh, dear!" said this poor Tilly to herself, "that South American gown, I suppose, proves that she must be that Smithson man's daughter; but grandmother was right,--she is innocent of the facts of the case, of that there can be no doubt,--and we must be good to her, and now is the time to begin,--this very minute, when Agnes is planning what hateful thing she can do next."

Fired by this thought, Tilly sprang to her feet, and, casting a glance of scorn and contempt at Agnes, slipped her hand over Peggy's arm and said,--

"Come, Peggy, let's go over to the other end of the piazza and walk up and down; it's much pleasanter there."

Warm-hearted Tilly's intentions were excellent; but her look of contempt, her meaning words, instead of cowing and controlling Agnes, only roused her to deeper anger, which resulted in an action that probably had not been premeditated even by her jealous and bitter spirit. Tilly will never forget that action. It was just as she was turning away with Peggy, when she saw that angry face barring her way, when she heard those ominous words, "Miss Smithson," and then--and then that outstretched hand thrusting forth to Peggy that fluttering, dreadful slip of paper!

CHAPTER V.

But another hand than Peggy's snatched at the fluttering paper. "What is it, what does it mean?" demanded Peggy, as a gusty breeze tore the paper from Tilly's trembling fingers.

"Yes, and what do you mean, Miss Tilly Morris, by snatching what doesn't belong to you?" cried Agnes, shrilly, as she started off to capture the flying paper, that, eluding her, blew hither and thither in a tantalizing way, and at last, falling at the feet of Will Wentworth, was picked up by him as he came out of the hall.

"It is mine, it is mine," shrieked Agnes; "keep it for me."

But Tilly, who was nearer to him, whispered agitatedly,--

"No, no, Will; don't give it to her,--she is--she means--"

"Mischief, I see," whispered back Will, with a swift, intelligent glance at Tilly.

"And if you wouldn't read it until--until I see you--oh, if you wouldn't!"

Will looked at Tilly with wonder. This was certainly something more serious than common. What was it,--what was the trouble?

But Agnes was by this time close upon him, reaching up her hand and crying, "Give it to me, Will, give it to me!"

But Will laughingly thrust the paper into his pocket, and answered,--

"No, I'll keep it for you, and give it to you later; I don't think it would be safe now. There's so much thunder in the air it might be struck by lightning."

"It might be snatched or stolen, I dare say," said Agnes, with a significant look at Tilly; "and you may keep it for me until later in the evening, and--read it at your leisure. It's a very interesting collection of facts."

"Tum, tum, ti tum," suddenly struck up the band in the hall.

"Eight o'clock!" cried Agnes, in astonishment.

"Yes, the ball's begun," said Will, nodding and smiling; "and if you'll excuse me," lifting his cap, "I'll go and get into my dancing shoes."

Agnes tried to smile in response; but a little pang of disappointment thrilled her as he left her without asking her for a dance. But he would later, of course,--later, when he would hand her her property, that collection of "facts," and by that time he would have read these "facts." She wouldn't need to risk any words of her own in accusation after that,--which conclusion shows very plainly that Miss Agnes had been sufficiently impressed with Tilly's warning to hold her peace.

That she had not flaunted the newspaper cutting before the eyes of others in the house also shows that the accident of the moment and her hot anger had, in the one instance only, overcome her caution.

But Tilly did not know all this, and her anxiety increased after she had heard those words to Will, "Read it at your leisure."

Peggy, too, had heard those words, though it was quite clear she had not heard that other word,--that dreadful name of Smithson; for, "What is it all about, that bit of paper?" she asked Tilly innocently, as Agnes and Will disappeared in the hallway; and Tilly said to her imploringly,--

"Don't ask me now, Peggy,--don't, that's a dear; I can't stand any more now."

And then and there Peggy answered, "I won't, I won't, you dear Tilly; I won't say another thing about it, and we won't think about it--" And then and there "Tum, tum, ti tum" burst forth the band in Strauss's "Morgen Blaetter" waltzes.

"Oh, how I love the 'Morgen Blaetter!'" cried Peggy. "Come, let us get into the dancing-hall as soon as possible. Where's auntie? Oh, there she is, talking with your pretty grandmother."

The next minute auntie and grandmother were sitting side by side in the dancing-hall, watching the two girls as they kept step to that perfect waltz music.

"Isn't it just lovely!" sighed Peggy.

"Lovely!" echoed Tilly.

"And how we suit each other! our steps are just alike."

"Just alike," echoed Tilly; whereat they both laughed, and a little silence between them followed, and then--

"There's Agnes dancing with Tom Raymond," suddenly exclaimed Tilly. "I wonder--"

"Don't wonder or worry about Agnes now, when we are tuned to the 'Morgen Blaetter' music," said Peggy. "'Music has charms to soothe the savage breast,' somebody has written, you know; and--and," with a soft little laugh, "it may soothe the breast of this savage Agnes."

Tilly echoed the soft little laugh, but she could not dismiss Agnes from her mind. She could not cease to wonder what it was she was talking about so earnestly with Tom Raymond,--to wonder if she had told, or was telling him at that very moment, of "Smithson, alias Smith."

And while poor Tilly wondered and worried, there was Peggy, the unconscious centre of all the wonder and worry, lifting up a radiant face of enjoyment as she floated along to the music of the "Morgen Blaetter." Tom Raymond, catching sight of this radiant face, said to himself,--

"I wonder if she's engaged for the next dance. I'll ask her the minute this is over."

The two girls were standing near their two chaperones when Tom came up, and with an odd sort of shyness, asked,--

"Are you engaged for the next dance, Miss--Miss Smith?"

Tilly's heart gave a jump as she noted Tom's sudden confusion and hesitation at this "Miss Smith," for it brought back to her his strange expression at the first sight of Peggy, and his question, "Is that the girl--the Miss Smith you were talking about?" and then his odd, chuckling laugh.

Peggy, too, had regarded Tom at that moment with a puzzled observation, as if she wondered if she had seen him before; and now, as Tom hesitated and bungled at the "Miss Smith," Peggy's own manner showed signs of consciousness, if not of embarrassment. Oh, oh! what could it all mean but that he had known everything from the first? "And I fancied at the first he acted as he did because he thought she wasn't quite fine enough; and all the time he knew she was this Miss Smithson, and was keeping it to himself, and, knowing that, he's going to ask her to dance with him now! Oh, what a good fellow he is, and what injustice I've done him!" concluded Tilly. "If only Will now, when he finds out--"

It was just then that a voice called softly from the open window behind her, "Miss Tilly, Miss Tilly!" and there was Will beckoning to her. "What shall I do with that paper?" he whispered, as Tilly turned. "I expect Agnes to be after me for it as quick as she catches sight of me again."

The window was a long French window, and Tilly stepped out and joined him upon the piazza. "Come around here where nobody can see or overhear us," she said. He followed her down the steps to a sheltered rustic seat.

"You haven't read it?" she asked.

"Read it? No!" Will answered a little huffily. "You asked me not to until I had seen you."

Tilly colored, and then, "You are a gentleman!" she burst out vehemently.

"Well, I hope so," Will answered.

"And so is Tom Raymond. I had done him such an injustice; but he's turned out so different from what I supposed he was. Oh, he's just splendid! and if you--" But here--I'm half ashamed to record it of my plucky little Tilly--here, suddenly overcome by all the excitement she had been through, Tilly broke down and began to cry.

"Oh, don't! I wish you wouldn't, now! Oh, I say!" cried Will, in boyish embarrassment.

Poor Tilly checked her sobs by a vigorous effort; but tears continued to flow, and she fumbled vainly for her handkerchief to dry them.

"Here, here, take mine," said Will, hastily thrusting the cambric into her hand; "and don't you bother another bit about Agnes and her tantrums. I'll burn her old paper if you say so, and I won't read it at all."

"Oh, yes, yes, you'll have to read it now. She'll ask you,--she'll tell you. Yes, read it, read it, Will. I know you'll pity Peggy, as grandmother and I do."

Thus adjured, Will drew the bit of paper from his pocket.

Tilly forgot her tears as she watched Will's face. He read it twice. At first there was an entire lack of comprehension; at the second reading a look of shocked understanding, and, bringing his fist down upon his knee, he exclaimed,--

"And Agnes was going to fling this bombshell straight at that poor thing!"

Then Tilly knew that Will was on the right side; that he pitied Peggy, and that he would agree with all that grandmother had said about her and her innocence and ignorance of real facts. This estimate of Master Will's sympathy was not a mistaken one. He not only agreed with grandmother about Peggy's innocence and ignorance, but in grandmother's kind conclusion "that they must be good to her."

"But what did you mean about Tom? What has he done to make you think so much better of him?" Will asked curiously.

While Tilly was enlightening him upon this point, Tom's voice was heard saying, "Oh, here they are," and Tom himself came round the clump of sheltering bushes accompanied by Peggy. And "We've been looking for you everywhere," said Peggy. "We've just had another of the Strauss waltzes, and the next thing is the 'Lancers;' and we want you and Tilly--"

"Will Wentworth, I want my property, if you please; that paper I gave you to keep for me," a very different voice--a high, sharp voice that the whole four recognized at once--interrupted here.

Tilly started, and turned pale.

"Don't be frightened, Tilly, she sha'n't have it," whispered Will.

Agnes flushed resentfully as she came forward and saw the confidential friendliness of the little group. For "that girl" she had been neglected and disregarded like this! Not a moment longer would she bear such insults. It was all nonsense,--all that stuff about being prosecuted for showing up facts. She would be stopped by that foolishness no longer. She would first take her stand boldly, and let everybody know what a fraud this Miss Smith was. These were some of the wild thoughts that leaped up out of the bitter fountain in Agnes's distorted mind at that instant, and her voice was sharper than ever as she again said,--

"I want my property,--the paper I gave you to keep for me."

Will had risen to his feet, and answered very coolly, "I can't give it to you."

"What do you mean? Have you lost it?"

"No, but I can't give it to you."

"Have you read it?"

"Yes, and that's the reason I don't give it to you. I know if I should you would--"

"Probably give it to Miss Smithson," cried Agnes, shrilly. "Miss Smithson," going toward Peggy, "I--"

"Oh, Peggy, Peggy, come with me. We're all your friends,--grandmother and I and Will and Tom; and we know how sweet and innocent you are. Oh, Peggy, come, come, and don't listen to her!" burst forth Tilly, in an agony of pity and horror, as she put an arm around Peggy to draw her away.

But Peggy was not to be drawn away.

"What in the world is the matter? What is it all about? What do you mean, Tilly, dear, by 'innocent'? What has she," glancing at Agnes disdainfully "been getting up against me?"

"Oh, Peggy, Peggy, don't!" moaned Tilly.

"Well, this is rich," laughed Agnes, jeeringly. "Nobody has been getting up anything against you, Miss Smithson."

"What do you mean by calling me Miss Smithson? That isn't my name."

"Oh, isn't it?" derisively. "How long since did you change it for Smith?"

"I have never changed it for Smith."

"Oh, I believe that 'Miss Smith' is down on the hotel register, and you answer to that name."

CHAPTER VI.

"I beg your pardon," said Peggy, looking at Agnes with great scorn. "'Mrs. Smith and niece' are down on the register. It was the clerk who registered us in that way, and all of you seemed to take it for granted that *my* name must be Smith also. Perhaps I ought to have corrected the mistake at once; but after I overheard that conversation on the piazza, and--saw somebody examining the register a few minutes later" glancing away from Agnes with a smile at Will, who looked rather sheepish--"after that I thought I'd let the mistake go until the rest of the family arrived, it was so amusing."

"Oh," retorted Agnes, "this all sounds very straight and pretty, but I dare say you've got used to telling such stories. Perhaps you'll tell us now what name you do call your own, and if it is by that those South American friends you write to are known."

"Perhaps Mr. Tom Raymond will tell you," answered Peggy, quickly. "I've thought for some time that he might be one of the Tennis Club that came out to Fairview at my brother's invitation last summer, and I thought he suspected who I was, and--and wouldn't tell because--because he saw, just as I did, what fun the mistake was. But now, if he will, he can introduce me--to my friends, Tilly and Will Wentworth, as--"

"Miss Pelham! Miss Margaret Pelham!" shouted Tom, before Peggy could go any further.

"Pelham!" cried Tilly, in a dazed way.

"Pelham!" repeated Will.

"Yes, Pelham! Pelham!" exclaimed Tom, exultantly, flinging up his cap with a chuckle of delighted laughter.

"And you're not--you're not the daughter of that dreadful Smithson?" burst forth Tilly, in a little transport of happy relief.

"'That dreadful Smithson'? Who is he, and who said I was his daughter?"

"**She** said it," roared Will, darting a furious look at Agnes; "and she cooked it all up out of this," suddenly pulling the paper from his pocket.

"Give it to me!" cried Agnes, breathlessly, springing forward to snatch the paper from his hand.

"No, no, you wanted me to give it to Miss Smith a minute ago, and now I'll give it to--Miss Pelham, and let her see what you've wanted to circulate about the house," answered Will.

"I--I--if I happened to notice it before the rest of you--and--and thought that it might be this Miss Smith--"

"That it **must** be! you insisted," broke in Will.

"With all that about the change of name, and the age of the girl, and--and--the 'South America' I saw on the blotting-pad, and the South American dress," went on Agnes, incoherently,--"if I happened to be before you, you thought afterward, I know you did, that it might be; and--"

"With a difference, with a difference!" suddenly rang out Peggy Pelham's clear young voice in tones of indignation. She had read the newspaper slip; and there she stood, scorn and indignation in her face as well as in her voice. "Yes, with a difference," she went on vehemently. "If they thought it might be, after you had paraded the thing before them, you," with a renewed look of scorn, "thought it **must** be, because you wanted it to be, because you had got to hating me. Oh, I can see it all now,--everything, everything; how you patched things together, even to that blotting-pad which I had used after directing my letter to my uncle, Berkeley Pelham, who lives in Brazil. Oh, to think of such prying and peering," with a shudder, "and to think of such enmity, anyway, all for nothing! I've heard of such enmity, but I never believed in it, for I never met it before. And all this time there was Tilly Morris,--oh, Tilly," whirling rapidly about, "what a dear, brave, generous, faithful little thing you've been," the ringing voice faltering, "for in spite of--even this--this dreadful Smithson, you stuck to me and tried to shield me."

"Oh, I knew, and so did grandmother, that you were innocent, whatever might just possibly have happened to--to--"

"Mr. Smithson--" And Peggy began to laugh. But the laugh ended in something like a sob, and she hurriedly hid her face on Tilly's shoulder. When an instant after she looked up, it was to see that Agnes had disappeared.

"Yes, the enemy has fled," said Tom Raymond. "The minute you dropped your eyes she was off. We might have stopped her, Will and I, but there wasn't much left of her. Oh, oh, oh! isn't she finished off beautifully, though?" and Tom gave way at last to the hilarity he had so long manfully repressed.

"Finished off! I should say so!" cried Will, joining in Tom's laughter.

"And to think that you were a Pelham,--one of Agnes's wonderful Pelhams all the time," put in Tilly, still with an air of bewilderment.

"And am now," laughed Peggy. "Oh, Tilly, you are such a dear!"

"One of Agnes's wonderful Pelhams!" shouted Tom. "Guess she won't be in a hurry to set up a claim to 'em now!" and Tom burst out again in wild chuckles of hilarity.

"And I never saw her, and I don't believe she ever met one of us before," cried Peggy.

"She told Amy that she didn't know the Pelhams yet, but that her Aunt Ann did, and her aunt was coming next month and would introduce her to them when they arrived," said Tilly, with a demure smile.

"Well, she'll probably like my sister Isabel's Skye terrier, with its fine name of Prince, much better than she does my poor little plebeian doggie, with its vulgar name of Pete," remarked Peggy, her eyes twinkling with fun.

"Oh, Peggy, to think of your hearing all that talk about the dog and everything."

"And everything? I should say so!" cried Will, starting up and looking rather red as he recalled his own words.

"Yes, and everything,--all about the dogs and the difference between the Wentworths and the Pelhams," took up Peggy, dimpling with smiles.

"Oh, I say now," began Will.

"Yes, you may say now just what you did then. I liked it,--I liked it. It was sensible and plucky of you, and it was such fun. Oh, when I think that but for auntie and me coming on ahead of the rest, and without a maid, and the hotel clerk writing only 'Mrs. Smith and niece' in the register, I should never have had all these wonderful experiences, and never have known what a friend my Tilly could be,-- when I think of all this, I want to dance a jig, just such a jig as they are playing this minute;" and up she jumped, this smiling Peggy, and, catching Tilly in her arms, went waltzing down the path with her toward the hall from whence floated the gay strains of the "Lancers."

But what was that sound,--that long-drawn, jubilant sound that suddenly rang over and above the dance music?

"Ta-ra, ta-ra, ta-ra-a-a-a," rang the clear, piercing notes; and out from halls and offices and parlors came a little flock of folk to see that most interesting of arrivals at a summer resort,--a coaching-party. "Ta-ra, ta-ra, ta-ra-a-a-a," wound the coach horn; and up the carriage drive rattled a superb vehicle, drawn by four superb gray horses. The long summer daylight yet lingered, and showed the faces of the party atop of the coach.

"It's the Pelham team, and that's young Berk Pelham holding the reins," said a bystander.

Dora and Amy Robson, who had run out with the others from the dancing-hall, caught Tom Raymond as he was passing them; and Dora whispered,--

"Are they the Pelhams,--Agnes's Pelhams?"

"'Agnes's Pelhams'? Oh, oh!" gurgled Tom, nearly choking with suppressed laughter. Then, "Yes, yes, Agnes's Pelhams; but where is Agnes? She ought to be here to welcome her Pelhams."

"She's gone to bed with a headache or something. She came in looking dreadfully a few minutes ago."

"I should think she might; she had had a blow."

"What do you mean? But, look, look! those Pelhams are speaking to that Smith girl."

"No, they're not."

"But they are, Tom; don't you see?"

"No, I don't see any of them speaking to a Smith girl, but I do see Miss Pelham speaking to--Miss Peggy Pelham."

Dora tossed her head impatiently. "What a silly joke!" she thought; but--but--

what was it that that tall young lady who had just jumped down from her top seat on the coach was saying?

"The minute I read your letter, Peggy, telling me of this little dance, Berk and I planned to drive over with the Apsleys and waltz a little waltz with you. Twenty miles in an hour and a half. Isn't that fine time? And you are looking so much better, Peggy, for the salt air, and away from all our racket. Mamma was wise when she sent you on ahead with auntie, but we're all coming to join you next week."

"Tom, Tom, you were not joking?" gasped Dora.

"When I said that girl was Peggy Pelham? Joking? No, it's a solid fact,--so solid it's knocked Agnes flat. Oh!" and Tom began to shake again; "it's too rich, it's too rich. Come over here away from the crowd, you and Amy, and let me tell you the whole story, and then you'll see what a blow Agnes has had."

Never had a narrator a more excitingly interesting story to tell, and never did narrator enjoy the telling more than Tom on this occasion; but though his hearers hung upon his words, these words were full of bitterness to them; and when at the close he flung his head back and said, "Isn't it the greatest fun?" Dora, out of her shame and mortification, cried,--

"Yes, fun to you,--to you and Will and Tilly, because you are on the right side of the fun; but I--we--are disgraced of course with Agnes. Oh, we've been just horrid--horrid, and such fools!"

"Well, I--I sort of forgot about you, that's a fact, in Agnes,--for it's her circus from the start; you and Amy," giving his little chuckling laugh, "are only humble followers, pressed into service, you know, by the ringmaster. The thing of it was, you hadn't sand enough to stand up against Agnes."

"And Tilly had," responded Dora, in a mortified tone.

"Oh, Tilly! Tilly's a trump, always and every time. She's on the right side of things naturally."

If Dora and Amy needed a still lower abyss of humiliation, they found it in this last sentence of Tom's, which showed them plainly what poor creatures he thought they were "naturally" to Tilly.

Before many hours the story of "that little Smith girl" was known throughout the house, and mothers and fathers and guardians heard with amazement that so serious a little drama had been going on without their slightest knowledge until this climax. One mother, however, Mrs. Robson, was more than amazed when she found what an influence Agnes had exerted over her daughter and niece.

"Don't offer as excuse that you didn't dare to tell me how things were going on for fear of offending Agnes Brendon," she said indignantly. "Didn't Tilly Morris dare to tell her grandmother?"

Everywhere it was Tilly Morris,--Tilly Morris, the kind, the brave, the honest! Even Mrs. Brendon, who came at last to know the fact, in her alarm and irritation assailed her daughter one day in the presence of the Robsons with these words,--

"Why couldn't you have behaved amiably and sensibly, like the little Morris girl? I don't see where you learned such suspicious, calculating, worldly ways of judging people and things?"

And then it was that Agnes turned upon her mother and gave utterance to these bitter, brutal truths,--

"I've learned them from the older people I've seen all my life,--the people who come to our house. They judge other people that they don't know anything about in just such calculating ways. They are always talking with you about this one or that one's social position, and they never make new acquaintances without finding out what set they belong to; and I was never allowed from a little girl to make acquaintances with any children whose mothers were not in the right set; and amiability and goodness had nothing to do with it,--nothing, nothing, nothing!"

THE EGG-BOY.

"Marge, Marge, here is the egg-boy!"

Marge dropped her book and ran to join her sister Elsie, who by this time was on the back piazza talking to a boy who had just driven up in a farm-wagon.

"We want two dozen more,--all nice big ones, and by to-morrow, for it is only three days before Easter, and they must be boiled and colored to be ready in season."

The boy stared. "Colored?" he repeated in a puzzled, questioning tone.

"Yes," answered Elsie, "colored. Don't you color eggs for Easter?"

"No."

"How queer! But you know about them, of course?"

"No, I don't."

"Not know about Easter eggs? Where in the world have you lived not to know about Easter? I thought everybody--"

"I do know about Easter," interrupted the boy, sharply. "All I said was that I didn't know about your colored eggs."

"Oh, well, I guess it is Episcopalians mostly who keep that old custom going in this part of the country, and I suppose your people are not Episcopalians, are they?"

"No."

"Well, *we* are, and we've lived in Washington, too, where everybody has colored eggs, and all the boys and girls there used to go to the egg-rolling party the Monday morning after Easter; and a good many of them go now."

"Egg-rolling party?" cried the boy, with such wide-open eyes of astonishment that Elsie and Marge both burst out laughing, whereat the boy flushed up angrily, and seizing the reins was starting off, when the cook called to him to wait until she had the butter-box ready for him to take back.

"Oh!" whispered Marge, "we've hurt his feelings, Elsie; it is too bad." Then she ran forward, and said gently: "'Tisn't anything at all strange that you didn't know about the rolling. Elsie and I didn't until we went to Washington to live, and saw the game ourselves, and had it explained to us; and I'll explain it to you. We had a lot of eggs boiled hard, and dyed all sorts of pretty flower colors and patterns; and these we took to the top of a little hill near the White House, and each one, or each party, started two or three or more eggs of different colors, and made guesses as to which color would beat. After the game was over, we exchanged the eggs we had, and gave away a good many to the poor children. Oh, it was great fun."

The boy laughed. "Fun! I should call it baby play!" he said derisively.

"Well, *you* can call it baby play if you like," returned Marge, with great dignity; "but the 'baby play' has come down through a good many years. It is an old Easter custom that was brought over from England by one of the early settlers at Washington."

"I--I didn't mean--I'm sorry--" began Royal, stammeringly; when--

"Royal! Royal Purcel!" called out a voice; and a little fellow scarcely more than six or seven years old came running up the driveway, and made a flying leap into the wagon.

"Do you belong to a circus?" cried Elsie.

"No; wish I did. I belong to Royal."

"Who is Royal?"

"Who is Royal?" repeated the child, making a cunning, impudent face at her.

"He means me. My name is Royal,--Royal Purcel; and he," nodding towards the child, "is my brother."

"Royal Purcel! **What** a funny name! It sounds--"

"Don't, Elsie," remonstrated Marge.

"It sounds just like Royal Purple," giggled Elsie, regardless of her sister's remonstrance.

Rhoda Davis, the cook, coming out just then with the butter-box, Royal thrust it hastily into the back of the wagon, and without another word or glance at the sisters, drove off at a headlong pace.

"Well, I never saw such a tempery boy as that in my life," said Elsie. "A boy that can't take a joke I don't think is much of a boy."

"Them Purcels allers was pretty peppery, and I guess they're more'n ever so now," said Rhoda.

"Why?" asked Marge.

"Why? Because they used to be the richest farmers about here. They owned pretty nigh all Lime Ridge once. Now they hain't got nothin' but that little Ridge farm. It's a stony little place, and how they manage to get a livin' off of it beats me."

"How'd they happen to lose so much?"

"Oh, the boy's father took to spekerlatin', and then some banks they had money in bust up."

"Well, he needn't fly up at everything because he isn't rich," said Elsie. "That's regular cry-baby fashion. He's a royal purple cry-baby, that's what he is, and I mean to call him that, see if I don't;" and Elsie laughed in high glee as this mischievous idea struck her. And while she and her sister were discussing Royal and his temper, Royal was discussing that very temper with himself.

"To think of my being such a fool as to show mad before those girls. I'm a regular sissy," was his final conclusion as he drove down the road.

The next morning, bright and early, he was up at the Lloyds' with two dozen fine big eggs. "As handsome a lot of eggs as I ever see," commented Rhoda, as she took them in.

"Are they going to color them all?" asked Royal.

"I s'pose so. Here are some of their old ones. They've been b'iled as hard as stones. They'll keep forever;" and Rhoda handed out of the open window a little basket of colored eggs.

"But some of these are painted," said the boy, taking up an egg with a pattern of flowers on it.

"No, they ain't; they're jest colored in a dye-pot. Them that looks as if they was painted were tied up in a bit of figgered calico and b'iled, and when they come out of the b'iling they took the calico off, and there was the figgers set on the eggs. See?"

"Yes, I see;" and Royal turned the egg round thoughtfully for a moment, then suddenly put it down, and started off towards his wagon on a run.

"Land sakes!" called out Rhoda; "what's come to you all at once to set off like that?"

"Muskrats!" shouted Royal, with a laugh as he jumped into the wagon.

"Ben a-settin' traps for 'em, eh?"

Royal nodded as he went rattling down the driveway.

"Did Royal Purple bring the eggs?" asked Elsie Lloyd, a little later.

"His name ain't Purple; it's Purcel," corrected Rhoda, innocently.

Elsie giggled. "Well, did Royal **Purcel** bring the eggs?" she asked.

"Yes, there they be."

"Oh, oh! aren't they beauties?"

"They be; that's a fact," agreed Rhoda. "Royal, he's done his best for ye now, anyway. He's kind o' quick, like all the Purcels, but he's real accommodatin'."

"So he is, Rhoda, and I'll give him one of the prettiest eggs we turn out for being so 'accommodatin';' and we are going to have some extra pretty ones this time. See this now, and this, and this!" and Elsie whipped out of her pocket several bits of bright calico. One was a pattern of tiny rosebuds; another a little lily on a blue ground.

"The lily ones will be just lovely if they turn out well, and they will be the real Easter egg with that lily pattern," said Marge, enthusiastically.

By Saturday afternoon a goodly array of eggs of all colors and patterns were "ready for company," as Elsie and Marge expressed it; for on Saturday night a party of their friends were coming to them for a three days' visit. It was about an hour after these friends had arrived, and they were all hanging admiringly over the pretty display of eggs, that a box was brought in by one of the servants. It was neatly tied, and directed in a bold round handwriting to "Miss Elsie and Miss Marge Lloyd."

"What *can* it be?" said Marge, wonderingly.

"We'll open it and see," cried Elsie. And suiting her action to her word, she cut the string and lifted the cover; and there she saw six eggs undyed, but each painted delicately with a different design. On one was a cross with a tiny vine running from the base; on another a bunch of lilies of the valley; and another showed a little bough of apple blossoms. On the remaining three the subjects were strangely unusual,--a palm and tent, with a patch of sky; a bird with outstretched wings, soaring upward with open beak, as if singing in its flight; a cherub head with a soft halo about it.

"Oh! oh! oh!" exclaimed the girls, in a chorus; and, "Who *could* have painted them?" wondered Marge; and, "Who *could* have sent them?" cried Elsie.

In vain they hunted for card or sign of the donor. They could find nothing to give them the slightest clew.

"Perhaps, papa, it is Mr. Archer," said Marge at last, turning to her father. Mr. Archer was an artist friend.

"Oh, no, this isn't Archer's work; it's a novice's work, though very promising," her father replied.

"Cousin Tom's, then?"

"And too strong for Tom."

"Then it must be Jimmy Barrows."

"Well, it may be Jimmy. We shall know when he comes with Tom on Monday. It's bold enough for Jimmy, but I didn't think he had so much fancy."

And finally it was settled that it could be no other than Jimmy Barrows. Jimmy was a great friend of their cousin Tom; but while Tom was only an amateur artist, Jimmy was studying to be a professional one.

"It's such fun to have Jimmy do these, and send them without a word," said Elsie to her sister.

"Such a generous thing to do, too! I wonder if he would like some of **our** eggs as specimens? We might give him one of each kind."

"Oh, Marge, don't think of offering him those calico-colored things,--anybody who can paint like this!"

"Very well; but, Elsie, which one are you going to give to Royal Purcel?"

"To Royal Purcel?"

"Yes; don't you remember you told Rhoda you were going to give him one for being so accommodating?"

"Oh, I'd forgotten. Well, here, I'll give him this,--it's the very thing;" and Elsie snatched up a bright purple one.

"Oh, Elsie, don't!"

But Elsie fairly danced with glee as she cried, "I will, I will; it's the very thing,--royal purple to Royal Purple!"

The young visitors, when all this was explained to them, joined in the merriment; but Marge--kind, tender little Marge--hid away one of the blue and white lily eggs, to get the advantage of Elsie's mischief by bestowing **that** upon Royal.

But Royal was quite out of Elsie's thoughts by Monday morning. It was a beautiful morning; and by nine o'clock, when Tom and Jimmy Barrows arrived, the lawn and sloping knoll at the east of it were bright and dry with sunshine. On the piazza the various baskets of eggs were standing; only "Jimmy Barrows's gift" had been set aside as "too good to use."

"My! haven't you got a lot, though?" cried Tom, as he surveyed them. "But what are these in the box here?"

"Yes, what are they?" sparkled Elsie. "Ask Jimmy Barrows."

Jimmy, with a wondering expression on his face at this remark, came over and looked down at the treasured eggs. "Who did these?" he asked quickly.

"'Who did these?'" mimicked Elsie. "Oh, you needn't try that. We found you out at once, or *I* did."

"You think I painted 'em--I sent 'em?" queried Jimmy.

"Of course I do. Now, Master Jimmy--"

"Miss Elsie, just as true as I'm standing here, I never saw them before."

Elsie shook her head at him, but Jimmy did not see her. He was lifting the eggs and examining them.

"No, honest, I didn't paint 'em, Miss Elsie. I wish I had; but I can't do things like that--yet. I can draw as well, am a better draughtsman, maybe, but I haven't got the ideas. The fellow who did these has got a lot of original ideas."

Mr. Lloyd came forward here with great interest. "Did any of you," turning to Elsie and Marge, "ask who brought the box?"

"Yes," answered Elsie. "I asked Ann, and she said 'a bit of a boy brought 'em;' she didn't know who he was."

"Ask Rhoda to come here. She knows the neighborhood."

Rhoda came, and Mr. Lloyd put the matter before her. Had she any idea who the "bit of a boy" was?

"I didn't see him, but it might be Bert Purcel," answered Rhoda. "Folks get him to do errands sometimes. He's just drove up with his brother to bring the chickens. I'll send him 'round, and you can ask him."

"Did you leave a box here Saturday night?" Mr. Lloyd inquired pleasantly, when the boy stood before him.

The red lips began to frame a "No," then closed tightly together, while the slim little figure whirled about and made an attempt to leap over the piazza railing,--an attempt that would have been successful if one foot had not caught in a stout vine.

Royal, waiting in the wagon at the back porch, heard a sudden cry, and hurried to see what had happened. He found Bert scrambling to his feet, brisk and angry. The child made a dash towards his brother, and seized his hand.

"What's the matter?" asked Royal. No answer, but a renewed tug at his hand to draw him away.

"The little fellow tried to jump the piazza railing and fell," explained Mr. Lloyd, laughingly.

"Papa just asked him a question,--if he brought us a box Saturday night; and as he didn't want to answer, he ran," spoke up Elsie.

"I didn't, I jumped!" cried the child.

Everybody laughed.

"Can't *you* tell us?" asked Marge, looking at Royal. "***Did*** your brother bring it?"

"Yes," answered Royal, flushing up.

"And who sent it?" asked Elsie, impatiently. She waited a moment for an answer. As none came, she asked still more impatiently, "Do you **know** the person who sent it?"

"Yes," in a hesitating voice.

"Did the person tell you not to tell?"

"No," in the same hesitating voice.

"Then why in the world **don't** you tell? You've no right to keep it back like this. It is our affair, not yours, and so it is our right to know who it is. Don't you understand that we don't want people to send us things--presents--and not know anything about who it is?"

Royal looked startled, and the flush on his face deepened. Elsie thought she had conquered him, and chirped out an encouraging, "Come, now, who was it?" But to her surprise the boy flung up his head with an angry movement, and with a defiant glance at her said stubbornly,--

"I've a perfect right **not** to answer your question, and I sha'n't!"

"Well, of all the brazen--"

"Elsie!" warned her father, "don't say anything more."

"You'll let me say one thing more, papa. Rhoda told us that this boy was very accommodating, and he brought me such nice big eggs, I thought he was, and meant to give him something to show my appreciation, and I'd like to give it to him now. Here," taking something from her pocket, "give this to your brother," she said to little Bert, who stood eying her curiously. The child's hand opened involuntarily. Into it dropped a *royal purple* egg.

Royal saw and understood. "Give it back to her!" he cried.

Bert, feeling the passion in his brother's voice, drew off, and *flung* the egg with all his might at Elsie. Luckily for her, it missed its aim and whizzed past, striking some article with a breaking crash beyond her.

"Oh! oh! oh! it's fallen on the painted eggs!" cried Marge, "and," running forward, "it has spoiled the lovely cherub head; see, the shell is all cracked to pieces!"

"You horrid, wicked boys!" cried Elsie, in the next breath.

But Royal heard nothing of these comments. The moment he saw that Bert's recklessness had injured no one, he had turned away with him, and was now driving out of the yard, scolding the youngster roundly for his action, and not a little subdued himself at what might have been the result of it.

"Papa, I think they ought to be punished, and the big boy made to tell," exclaimed Elsie, when she found the two were out of her reach.

"What did you say was the name of the boys?" asked Jimmy Barrows, who had taken up the cross and vine egg, and was peering at it very closely.

"Purcel."

"Well, just look at this;" and with the tip-end of a tiny knife-blade Jimmy pointed out something in the delicate vined tendrils that had hitherto escaped notice. It was the name "R. Purcel," cunningly inwound in the tendrils. Every one crowded up to inspect this discovery.

"It must be some relation of the boy's, and that is why he felt he had a right to keep it secret," said Mr. Lloyd.

"But it was Royal's present, whatever relation he got to paint the eggs for him, for it was only Royal who knew about *our* eggs; and this is the way we've paid him!" cried Marge, with a glance of indignant reproach at Elsie.

"I don't think he got anybody to do it for him; I--I think he did it himself," spoke up Jimmy.

"Royal Purcel! that--that farm-boy?" shrieked Elsie.

"Yes," answered Jimmy. "I thought so all the time, when you--when he was standing under--under your questioning fire." And Jimmy laughed.

"But how did he learn?" cried Elsie, in astonishment.

"I don't think the boy has had much instruction," said Jimmy. "I think he has great natural talent, and has had very little opportunity to study." Jimmy was now peering at the palm and tent egg, and, "See, here's the name again, in this thready grass," he said, "and he has probably marked all the eggs in this cunning way."

Jimmy was right. On the bird's wing, amid the lily leaves, and on the apple bough, they also found "R. Purcel" hidden deftly from casual observation.

Elsie was silent as, one after another, these discoveries were made. Finally she could contain herself no longer, and burst out,--

"To think of his painting all these beautiful things and giving them to us,--to me, when I've been such a horrid little cat to him! Oh, papa, I must do something,--I just must!"

"Well, I should think it would become you to say you are sorry and to thank him," said Mr. Lloyd, smiling.

"But, papa, I want to take the pony-carriage and go after him, and ask him to come back to the egg-rolling; and if Jimmy Barrows will go with me--"

"I'd be delighted, Miss Elsie."

"He'd make it easier,--he'd know what to say, and Royal would know what to say to him. The others will excuse us; we won't be long. Oh, may I--may we, papa?"

"Well, as you seem to have settled everything, I don't see but I must--"

But Elsie did not wait to hear more. She knew she had not only her father's consent, but his approval, and was off like a flash to order the carriage.

If the Lloyds had been better acquainted in Lime Ridge, Royal's work would not have been such a great surprise to them. A good many of the Lime Ridge people could have told them of the boy's talent, and how it had been discouraged by his family. There was no money now to support and educate him in that direction, and it had been arranged with an old friend who was in the wool business that the boy should go into his employ as soon as he had graduated from the Lime Ridge High School. This was considered a very lucky prospect for him, but Royal hated it. From a little fellow he had shown a great love for pictures, and had covered every scrap of paper he could find with crude drawings.

When he was eight years old, a visitor had given him a box of paints and brushes. Two years later he had become acquainted with an artist who was staying a few weeks at Lime Ridge, and went with him on his sketching-tramps. With him he learned something about an artist's methods, and received from him as a parting gift, various artist's materials that he had made industrious use of.

The whim of painting the eggs and sending them to the sisters had come to him as a sort of apology to them for his exhibition of temper, and he had no idea that his name, so palpable to his artist eye, would escape their observation as it did. He expected his gift and its motives to be recognized at once. Instead, he was questioned as if he were nothing but an ignorant errand-boy; and, bitterest of all, even when he had confessed to a knowledge of the giver, the possibility of his being the painter himself was not for a moment suspected. But while he stood leaning over the farm-gate thinking these bitter thoughts, a stout little pony was bringing him what he little dreamed of. "Catch me ever going amongst 'em again,--an overbearing lot of city folks," he was saying to himself, when, patter, patter, patter, round the turn of the road came the stout little pony, and before the boy could make a movement to get away, Elsie Lloyd had jumped from the wagon, and stood in front of him.

"I've come to ask you to go back with us, and forgive me for being such a horrid little cat to you. I didn't understand. I thought--" and then in a perfect jumble of words Elsie went on, and poured forth her contrition and explanation, at the same time introducing Jimmy Barrows, who knew just what to say, and said it with such effect that Royal's spirits went up with a bound, and almost before he knew to what he had consented, he was sitting on the little back seat of the phaeton, talking with these "city folks" as if they were his best friends, as they turned out to be.

All this happened four or five years ago, and to-day where do you suppose Royal Purcel is, and what do you suppose he is doing? In Mr. Carr's mills, learning to pick and buy wool?

Not he. He is in Paris with Jimmy Barrows, studying hard, and supporting himself by making business illustrations for various newspapers. It is humble work, but it serves for his support while he is preparing for higher things; and the "higher things" are not far off, for two or three of his sketches in oils have attracted the attention of the critics, and he has furnished a set of drawings for a child's book that has been well paid for and well spoken of. And Jimmy Barrows wrote home to Tom Lloyd the other day,--

"Royal is going to be a howling success, as I always prophesied; but what a time your uncle and I had to persuade his family of this possibility, and to get him off from that wool-picking! But I guess they began to believe we were right when this spoiled wool-picker wrote them last week that he'd paid the last cent of his indebtedness to Mr. Lloyd. Houp-la!"

"'A howling success'! And it's all through me," laughed Elsie, as she read this portion of Jimmy's letter; "for if I hadn't eaten humble-pie, and run after Master Royal that morning, he would not have met Jimmy Barrows, and might have been wool-picking to this day. Yes; it's all through me and my humble-pie. Houp-la!"

MAJOR MOLLY'S CHRISTMAS PROMISE.
CHAPTER I.

"Never had a Christmas present?"

"No, never."

"Why, it's just dreadful! Well, there's one thing,--you *shall* have one this year, you dear thing!" and Molly Elliston flung down the Christmas muffler she was knitting, and stared at her visitor, as if she could scarcely believe what she had just confessed to her. The visitor laughed, showing a beautiful row of small white teeth as she did so. She was a charming little maiden of twelve or thirteen, this visitor,--a charming little maiden with the darkest of dark hair that hung in a thick shining braid tied at the end with a broad red ribbon. Molly Elliston thought she was a beauty, as she looked at her dimpled smiling face,--a beauty, though she *was* an Indian. Yes, this charming little maiden was an Indian, belonging to what was once a great and powerful tribe. When, three years ago, Molly Elliston had come out to the far Northwest with her mother to join her father on his ranch, she had thought she should never feel anything but aversion to an Indian. Molly was then seven years old, and had always lived at some military post, for her father had been an army officer until the three years before, when he had given up his commission to enter into partnership with his brother upon a sheep and cattle ranch. A few miles from this ranch was an Indian reservation. The tribe that occupied it had for a long time been quite friendly with white people, and were therefore not altogether unwelcome neighbors to the Ellistons. Molly thought they were very welcome, indeed, when one day, in the third summer of her ranch life, she made the acquaintance of this pretty Wallula, who was not only pretty, but very intelligent, and of a loving disposition that responded gladly to Molly's friendly advances.

"But to think that you've never had a Christmas present!" exclaimed Molly again, as Wallula's laugh rippled out. "If I'd *only* known you the first year we came! But I'll make it up *this* year, you'll see; and oh! oh!" clapping her hands at a sudden thought, "I know--I know what I'll do! Tell you?" as Wallula clapped *her* hands and cried, "Oh, tell me, tell me!" "Of course I sha'n't tell you; that would spoil the whole. Why, that's part of the fun that we don't tell what we are going to do. It is all a secret until Christmas eve or Christmas morning."

"Yes, I know,--Metalka told me; but I forgot."

"Of course your sister must have known all about Christmas after she came back from school. Why didn't *she* make you a Christmas present, then, Lula?"

"Metalka?" A cloud came over the little bright face. "Metalka didn't stay long after she came back. She didn't stay till Christmas; she went 'way--to--to heaven."

"Oh!"

"If Metalka had stayed, I might have gone to school this year."

"I thought you *had* been to school, Lula."

"Oh, no! only to little school out here summers,--little school some ladies made; and Metalka tole me--taught me--showed me ev'ry day after she came back--ev'ry day, till--til she--went 'way. I can read and write and talk, talk, talk, all day in English,"--smiling roguishly, then more seriously and anxiously. "Is it pretty fair English,--white English,--Major Molly?"

"'White English'!" laughed back Major Molly. "You are such fun, Lula. Yes, it's pretty fair--white English."

Lula dimpled with pleasure, then sighed as she said, "If I could go 'way off East to Metalka's school, two, three, four, five year, as Metalka did, then I could talk splen'id English, and I could make heap--no, all sort things, and help keep house nice, and cook like Metalka."

"But why don't you go, Lula?"

"Why don't I? Listen!" and Wallula bent forward eagerly. "I don't go because my father won't have me go. Metalka went. When she first came back, she was so happy, so strong. She was going to have everything white way, civ--I can't say it, Maje Molly."

"Do you mean civilized?"

"Yes, yes; civ'lized--white way. And she worked, she talked, she tried, and nobody'd pay much 'tention but my father. The girls, some o' them, wanted to be like her; but the fathers and mothers would n' help, and some, good many, were set hard 'gainst it; and then there was no money to buy white people's clothes, they said. It took all the money was earned to pay big 'counts up at agency store, where Indians bought things,--things to eat, you know; so what's the use, they said, to try to live white ways when everything was 'gainst them, and they stopped trying; and Metalka was so dis'pointed, for she was going do so much,--going help civ-civ'lize. She was so dis'pointed, she by-'n'-by got sick--homesick, and just after the first snow came, she--she went 'way to heaven. And that's why my father won't have me go to the school. He say it killed Metalka. He say if she'd stayed home, she'd been happy Indian and lived long time. He say Indian got hurt; spoiled going off into white man's country."

"How came he to let your sister go, Lula?"

"Metalka wanted to go so bad. She'd heard so much 'bout the 'way-off schools from some white ladies up at the fort one summer, and my father heard too. A white off'cer tole him if Indian wanted to know how to have plenty to eat, plenty ev'rything like white peoples, they must learn to do bus'ness white ways, be edg'cated. So he let Metalka go; *he* could n' go, he too old; but Metalka could go and learn to read all the books and the papers and keep 'counts for him, so 't he'd know how to deal with white men. When Metalka first took 'count for him, after she came back, my father so pleased. He'd worked hard all winter hauling wood, and killing elk and deer for the skins; and my mother 'n' I had made bewt'ful moccasins and gloves out o' the skins, all worked with beads; and so he'd earned good deal money, and he 'd kept 'count of it all,--*his* way, and 't was honest way; and kept 'count, too, what he'd had out of agency store; and Metalka understood and reckoned it all up, and said he 'd have good lot money left after he'd paid what he owed at the store. But, Maje Molly, he didn't! he didn't! They tole him he owed *all* his money, and when he said they'd made mistake, and showed 'em Metalka's 'counts, they laughed at him, and showed him big book of *their* 'counts, and tole him Metalka didn't know 'bout prices o' things. Then he came home and said: 'What's the use going to white people's schools to learn white people's ways, when white people can come out to Indian country and tell lies 'bout prices o' things?' And that's the way 't is ev'ry time, my father say; the way 't was before Metalka went to school. The bad white trader comes out to Indian country to cheat Indians. *He* knows white prices, but he don't tell Indian white prices; he tell Indian two, three time more price. That's what my father say. And Metalka, when she see it all, she so disjointed, she never get over it, and my father say it killed her, like arrow shot at her."

"But your father doesn't think all white people bad; he doesn't dislike all their ways?"

"No; it's only white traders he thinks bad, and the white big chiefs who break promises 'bout lands. He like white ways that Metalka brought back, and he built nice log house to live in instead of tepee, 'cause Metalka wanted it; and he like all you here, Maje Molly, 'cause you good to me. But, Maje Molly"--and here the little bright face clouded over--"my mother say *all* white peoples forget, and break promises to Indians."

"No, no, they don't, Lula; they don't, you'll see. *I* sha'n't forget; *I* sha'n't break *my* promise, you'll see,--you'll see, Lula. On Christmas eve I shall send you a Christmas present, sure,--now remember!" answered Molly, vehemently.

CHAPTER II.

It was the day before Christmas,--a beautiful, mild day, very unlike the usual winter weather in the far West. At the Ellistons' windows hung wreaths of pine, and all about on tables and chairs tempting-looking packages were lying. Some of these were from their military friends, and most of them were directed to "Major Molly," the name that had been given to Molly when she was a little tot of a thing, and the pet of the fort where she lived. On this Christmas day, as she watched her mother fold up the pretty bright tartan dress that was to be her Christmas present to Wallula, she said gleefully,--

"Don't forget, mamma, to write on the box, 'Wallula's Christmas present from Major Molly.'"

It had been Molly's intention to have Wallula to tea on Christmas eve, and then and there to bestow upon her the pretty gift. But invitations to dine at the fort had frustrated this plan, and so it was arranged that Barney McGuire, one of the ranchmen, should come up and carry the box over to the reservation late that afternoon;

and as the short winter day progressed, and Molly found that she must have a little more time to finish off the table-cover she wanted to take up to the Colonel's wife, she said to her mother,--

"Instead of going on with you and papa at five o'clock, let Barney escort me to the fort after he leaves Wallula's present; that will give me plenty of time to finish the cover, and plenty of time to get to the dinner in season."

"Very well," answered Mrs. Elliston; "but you must promise me to start with Barney as soon as he comes back for you, whether the cover is finished or not. You mustn't be late."

At five o'clock, when Captain Elliston and his wife rode off, Molly was working away at her cover with the greatest industry. Now and then, as she worked on, she glanced up at the clock. If everything went smoothly,--if the silk didn't knot or the lace didn't pucker,--she would be through long before Barney came back for her. But presently she thought, where *was* Barney. He ought to be there for the box by this time. She worked on a little longer, her ear alert for the sound of Barney's horse. At last she went to an upper window and looked out. She could see, even in the gathering dusk, a great distance from that window, away across toward the sheep-corrals and cattle-pens; but nobody was in sight. What did it mean? Barney was punctuality itself.

Five, ten, fifteen, twenty minutes more she worked with flying fingers, and still there was no sight or sound of Barney; but her work was finished, and now--now, what then?

There was only Hannah and John, the two house-servants, at hand. Hannah couldn't go, and John had strict orders never to leave the premises in Captain Elliston's absence. She looked at the clock; every second seemed an age. If Barney didn't come, if *no one was sent in his place*, her promise to Wallula would be broken, and Molly remembered Wallula's words, "My mother say all white peoples forget, and break promises to Indians;" and her own vehement reply, "*I* sha'n't forget; I sha'n't break *my* promise, you'll see, you'll see, Lula!" Break her promise after that! Never, never! Her father himself would say she must not,--would say that *somebody* must go in Barney's place, and there was nobody,--nobody to go but--herself!

"Yer goin' alone, yer mean, over to the Injuns!" demanded John, as Molly told him to bring her pony, Tam o' Shanter, to the door.

"Yes, yes, and right away, John; so hurry as fast as you can."

"Do yer think yer'd orter, Major Molly? Do yer think the Cap'n would like it?" asked John, disapprovingly.

"John, if you don't bring Tam 'round this minute, I'll go for him myself."

"'T ain't safe fur yer to go over there alone!" cried Hannah.

"Safe! I know the way, every inch of it, with my eyes shut, and so does Tam; and I know the Indians, and Wallula is my friend; and I told her she should have her present Christmas eve, sure, and I'm going to keep my promise. Now bring Tam 'round just as quick as you can."

John obeyed, though with evident reluctance, and Hannah showed her disapproval by scolding and protesting; but they had both of them lived on the frontier for years, and their disapproval therefore was not what it might have been under different circumstances. Molly, they knew, could ride as well as a little Indian, and was familiar with every inch of the way, as she had said, and Wallula was her friend.

"And 't wouldn't 'a' done the least bit o' good to hev set myself any more against her. If I had, just as like as not the Cap'n would 'a' sided with her and been mad at me, for he thinks the Major's ekal to 'most anything," John confided to Hannah, as he brought the pony round.

The pony shied a little as Wallula's Christmas present was strapped to his back. But at Molly's whispered, "Tam! Tam! be a good boy. We're going to see Wallula,--to carry her something nice, just as quick as we can go," the little fellow whinnied softly, as if in response; and the next moment, at Molly's "Now, Tam," he started forward at his best pace,--a pace that Molly knew so well, and knew she could trust,--firm and even and assured, and gaining, gaining, gaining at every step.

"Good boy, good boy!" she said to him as he sped along. But as he began to hasten his pace, it occurred to her that it was only about half an hour's easy riding to the reservation, and that after leaving there she could easily reach the fort in another half-hour,--so easily that there was no need of hurrying Tam as she was doing; and she pulled him up with a "Take it easy, Tam dear." As she spoke, Tam flung up his head, pricked up his ears, and made a sudden plunge forward. What was it? What was the matter? What had he heard? He had heard what Molly herself heard in the next instant,--the beat of a horse's hoofs. But the minute it struck upon Molly's ear she said to herself, "It's Barney; for that's old Ranger's step, I know." Ranger was an old troop horse of her father's that Barney often rode. But in vain she tried to rein Tam in. In vain she said to him, "Wait, wait! It's Ranger and Barney, Tam!"

The pony snorted, as if in scorn, and held on his way. What **was** the matter with him? He was usually such a wise little fellow, and always knew his friends and his enemies. ***And he knew them now***! He was wiser than she was, and he scented on the wind something that spurred him on.

But, hark! What was that whirring, singing sound? Was that a new signal that Barney was trying? Was it--Whirr, s-st! Down like a shot dropped Tam's head, and like an arrow he leaped forward, swerving sideways to escape the danger he had scented,--the danger of a lariat flung by a practised hand.

Oh, Tam, Tam! fly now with all your speed, your mistress understands at last. She is a frontier-bred girl. She knows now that it is no friendly person following her, but some one who means mischief; and that mischief she has no doubt is the proposed capture of Tam, who is well known for miles and miles about the country as a wonderful little racer. Yes, Molly understands at last. She has **seen in the starlight** the lariat as it missed Tam's head, and she knows perfectly well that only Tam's speed and sure-footedness can save them. Her heart beats like a trip-hammer; but she keeps a firm hold upon the rein, with a watchful eye for any sudden inequalities of the road, while her ears are strained to catch every sound. Tam's leap forward had given him a moment's advantage, and he keeps it up bravely, his dainty feet almost spurning the ground as he goes on, gaining, gaining, gaining at every step. In a few minutes more they will be out of the reach of any lariat, then in another minute safe at Wallula's door.

In a few minutes! As this thought flashes through Molly's mind, wh-irr, s-st! cuts the still air again. Tam drops his head, and plunges forward.

Though the starlight is brighter than ever, Molly does not **see** the lariat, but there is something, something,--what is it?--that prompts her to fling herself forward face downwards upon Tam's mane; and the lariat that was about to drop over her head once more falls harmless to the ground, and Tam once more seems to know what danger has been escaped, and starts forward again with an exultant bound. They are almost there! Molly sees the smoke from the tepees of the reservation, and a light from a log cabin, and draws a breath of relief. But not yet, O brave little frontier girl, O gallant little steed, is the race won and the danger passed! Not yet, oh, not yet! for just ahead there is a treacherous pitfall which neither Tam nor his mistress sees,--a hollow that some little animal has burrowed out, and into this Tam plunges a forefoot, stumbles, and falls!

CHAPTER III.

"She *said*, 'I sha'n't forget; I sha'n't break *my* promise. You'll see, on Christmas eve, I shall send you a Christmas present, sure. Now remember.' On Christmas eve! And to-night is Christmas eve!"

Wallula had said this over and over to herself ever since the sun went down. She had kept count of the days from the day that Molly had made her that vehement promise. That promise meant so much to Wallula. It meant not merely a gift, but keeping faith, holding on, making real friends with an Indian girl. And her mother had said, "*She'll* forget, like the rest. White peoples always forget what they say to Indians." And her father had nodded his head when her mother said this. But Wallula had shaken *her* head, and declared with passionate emphasis more than once,--

"Major Molly will never forget,--never! You'll see, you'll see!"

Wallula had awakened very early that morning, and the minute she opened her eyes she thought, "This is the day before Christ's day. To-night, 'bout sundown, Major Molly'll keep her promise." All through the day this happy thought was uppermost. In the afternoon she followed Major Molly's instructions, and hung pine wreaths about the cabin.

The short afternoon sped on, and sundown came, and the gray dusk, and then the stars came out.

"Where's your Major Molly now?" asked the mother. There was a sharp accent in the Indian woman's voice, and a bitter expression on her face. But it was not for Wallula; it was for the white girl,--the Major Molly who, in breaking her promise to Wallula, had brought suffering upon her; for on Wallula's face the mother could see by this time the shadow of disappointment gathering. It made her think of Metalka. Metalka had gone amongst the white people. She had come back full of belief in them, and it was the white people's white traders with their lies and their broken promises that had hurt Metalka to death. There was only little Wallula left now. Was it going the same way with Wallula? These were some of the Indian mother's bitter resentful thoughts as she watched Wallula's face.

Wallula found it very hard to bear this watchfulness. She felt as if her mother were glad that her prophecy had proved true, that the white girl had broken her promise; but Wallula was wrong. Her mother's bitterness and resentment were the outcome of her anxiety. She would have given anything, have done anything, to have saved Wallula this suffering. If something would only happen to rouse Wallula, she thought, as she watched her. There had come a visitor to their cabin the other day,--the chief of a neighboring tribe. When he saw Wallula, he said he would come again and bring his little daughter. If he would only come soon! If he would only--But, hark! what was that? Was it an answer to her wish,--her prayer? Was he coming now--*now*? And, jumping to her feet, the woman ran to the door and flung it open. Yes, yes, it was in answer to her prayer; for there, over the turf, she could see a horse speeding towards her. It was coming at breakneck speed. "Wallula! Wallula!" she turned and called. An echo seemed to repeat, "Lula, Lula!" At that echo Wallula leaped up, and sped past her mother with the fleetness of a fawn, calling as she did so, "I'm coming, coming!" In the next instant the wondering woman saw her child running, as only an Indian can run, by the side of a jet-black pony whose coat was flecked with foam, and whose breath was well-nigh spent. As they came nearer into the pathway of light that the pine blaze sent forth from the open door, something that looked like a pennon of gold streamed out, and a clear but rather shaken voice cried, "Lula, Lula, I've kept my promise; I've kept my promise!"

The next moment the owner of the voice had slid from the pony's back into Wallula's arms, and Wallula was stroking the streaming golden hair, and crying jubilantly, "She's kept her promise, she's kept her promise!"

"Yes, I've kept my promise. I've brought your Christmas present. There it is in that box strapped across Tam. If somebody'll unstrap it and see to Tam, we'll go into the house, and I'll tell you what a race I've had. I can only stay a few minutes, for I must get to the fort if your father'll go with me. I don't dare to go alone now."

"To the fort?" asked Wallula, wonderingly.

"Yes, I'm going there to dinner; but let's go in. I'm so tired I can hardly stand;

and Tam--"

But as a glance showed her that Tam was being cared for, and that Wallula's mother was carrying the box into the house, Major Molly followed on with a sigh of relief, and, doffing the riding-suit that covered her dress, flung herself down before the blazing fire, and began to tell her story. When she came to the point where Tam stumbled and fell forward, she burst out excitedly,--

"Oh, Lula, Lula! I thought then I should never get here, and I don't know how we did it, Tam and I; I don't know how we did it, but I kept my seat, and I gave a great pull. I felt as strong as a man, and I cried, 'Tam! Tam! Tam!' and Tam,--oh, I don't know how he did it,--Tam got to his feet again, and then he flew, flew, *flew* over the ground. We'd lost a minute, and I expected every second the lariat would catch us sure after that, but it didn't, it didn't, and I'm here safe and sound. I've kept my promise, I've kept my promise, Lula."

"Yes, she kep' her promise, she kep' her promise!" repeated Wallula in glad triumphant accents, glancing at her mother, and at the tall gaunt figure of her father standing in the shadow of the doorway.

Wallula was a young girl, and this mystery of a Christmas-box was full of delight to her; but just then a greater delight--the joy of Major Molly's fidelity--made her forget everything else. But Molly did not forget. The minute she had finished her story she sprang to her feet, and produced the contents of the box. Wallula clapped her hands with delight when the pretty bright dress was held up before her.

"Just like Major Molly's,--just like Major Molly's! See! see!" she called out to her father and mother.

The mother nodded and smiled. The father's eyes lighted with an expression of deep gratification; then he leaned forward eagerly, and said to Molly,--

"Tell 'gain 'bout where you saw--heard--lar'yet."

"Just as we got to the little pine-trees where the old Sioux trail stops," answered Molly, promptly.

"Yah!" ejaculated the Indian, grimly, in a tone of conviction. Then, turning, he took down a Winchester rifle, slung it over his shoulder, and started towards the door, saying to Molly as he did so: "You stay here with Wallula. I go up to fort and tell 'em 'bout you."

"Oh, take me with you, take me with you!" cried Molly, jumping up.

The Indian shook his head. When Molly insisted, he said tersely: "No, not safe for little white girl yet. Maje Molly stay here till I come back."

Molly's face fell. Wallula stole up to her. "I got bewt'ful Chris'mas present for Maje Molly," she said softly. "Maje Molly stay see it with Wallula."

"You dear!" cried Molly, flinging her arm round Wallula.

The Indian father nodded his head vigorously, and his face shone with satisfaction. "Yes, yes!" he said. "Wallula take care you. You stay till I come back."

In looking at and trying on the "bewt'ful Chris'mas present,"--a pair of elaborately embroidered moccasins lined and bordered with rabbit fur,--and in dressing Wallula up in the tartan dress, the time flew so rapidly that long before Molly expected it the cabin door opened again, and the tall gaunt figure reappeared.

Behind it followed another figure. Molly ran forward as she saw it, and, "Papa, papa!" she cried, "I waited and waited for Barney, and he didn't come; and I couldn't bear for Lula not to have her Christmas present to-night, for I'd promised it to her to-night. She told me, when I promised, that white people always broke their promises to Indians, and I said over and over that *I* wouldn't break *my* promise; and I couldn't--I couldn't break it, papa."

"You did quite right, my little daughter,--quite right."

There was something in her father's manner as he said this, a seriousness in his voice and in his eyes, that surprised Molly. She was still more surprised when the Indian suddenly said,--

"She little brave; she come all 'way 'lone to keep promise, so she not hurt my Wallula. She make me believe more good in white peoples; so I go to fort,--I keep friends."

"You've been a friend indeed. I sha'n't forget it; we'll none of us forget it, Washo," said Captain Elliston; and he put out his hand as he spoke, and grasped the brown hand of the Indian in a warm friendly clasp.

At the fort everything was literally "up in *arms*,"--that is, set in order for business, and that meant ready for resistance or attack. Molly had lived most of her fourteen years at some Western military post, and she recognized at once this "order" as she rode in.

"What *did* it mean?" she asked again, as the Colonel himself met her and hurried her into the dining-room; and the Colonel himself answered her,--

"It means, my dear, that Major Molly has saved us from being surprised by the enemy, and that means that she has saved us from a bloody fight."

"I--I--" faltered Molly. Then like a flash her mind cleared, and she struck her little hand on the table and cried,--

"It was an Indian, an unfriendly Indian, who followed me, and Washo knew it when I told my story!"

"Yes, Washo knew it, and, more than that, he had known for some days that those particular Indians had been planning a raid upon us, and he didn't interfere; he didn't warn us because he had begun to think that we were all bad white traders, and he wouldn't meddle with these braves who proposed to punish us, though he wouldn't go on the war-path with them. But, Major Molly, when he heard your story, when he saw how one of us could be a little white brave in keeping a promise to an Indian, *for your sake* he relented towards the rest of us."

"And when he asked me to tell him where I first heard the lariat--"

"When he asked you that, he was making sure that it was his Sioux friends,--for he knew they were to send out a scout who would take exactly that direction."

"But why--why did the scout chase *me*?"

"He was after Tam, no doubt,--for this Sioux band is probably short of ponies, and Tam, you know, is a famous fellow,--and the moment the scout caught sight of him he would give chase."

"Did he get Ranger that way? And where, oh, where is poor Barney?"

"The probability is that the scout visited the corral first, and captured Ranger, who is almost as famous as Tam."

"But, Barney--oh, oh, *do* you think Barney has been killed?"

"We don't know yet, my dear. Your father has gone off to the ranch with a squad of men. He'll soon find out what's happened to Barney. And don't fret, my dear, about your father," seeing a new anxiety on Molly's face. "The raiders by this time have seen our signals, and have found out we're up and doing, and more than a match for them; so don't fret,--don't fret, any of you," turning to his wife and Mrs. Elliston. "I don't think there'll be so much as a skirmish."

And the Colonel was right. When the Indians saw the signals and the other signs of activity, they knew that their only chance of overcoming the whites by taking them unawares was gone. There were a few shots fired, but no skirmish; and by the time the moon rose, the fort scouts brought in word that the whole band had departed over the mountains. A few minutes after, when Captain Elliston rode in, the satisfaction was complete, for he brought with him the news of Barney's safety. Ranger, however, was gone. The Indian--or Indians, for there were two of them at that point--had succeeded in capturing him just as Barney had started out from the corral. A stealthy step, a skilful use of the lariat, and Barney was bound and gagged, that he might give no alarm; and all this with such quiet Indian alertness that a ranchman farther down the corral heard nothing.

So harmlessly ended this raid, that might have been a bloody battle but for Major Molly's Christmas promise!

POLLY'S VALENTINE.
CHAPTER I.

Polly was seven years old before she knew anything about valentines. This may seem very strange to most girls, for most girls have heard all about Valentine's Day by the time they are three or four, and have had no end of fun sending and receiving these friendly favors. But Polly didn't know a thing about them until she was seven. I'll tell you why. Polly was one of a number of children who lived in an Orphan's Home, and Polly herself was the youngest of the orphans.

One morning as she looked out of the window, she saw the postman suddenly surrounded by a whole flock of little girls, and heard one of them say, "Oh, *haven't* you got a valentine for me?" And then the whole flock cried, "And for me? and for me?" And the postman laughed good-naturedly, and, looking through his pack of letters, took out two or three quite big square envelopes, and handed them to one and another of the clamorous little crowd.

Polly, hearing and seeing all this, wondered what a valentine could be. She did not ask anybody the question, however, just then; but when the postman came around at noon, and she saw the same scene repeated, her curiosity could not be restrained any longer, and she started off to find Jane McClane,--for Jane was fourteen years old and knew everything, Polly thought.

Jane was in the linen-room mending a sheet when Polly found her, and being rather lonesome was quite willing to enter into conversation with any one who came along. But Polly's question made her open her eyes with surprise.

"A valentine?" she exclaimed. "You don't mean to say, Polly, you never heard of a valentine before?"

"No, never," answered Polly, feeling very small and ignorant.

"Well, to be sure," said Jane, "you're very little, and ain't 'round much, but I **should** have thought you'd have heard **somebody** say something about valentines before this; but you ain't much for listening and asking, I know."

"No," echoed Polly; "but I'm listening now."

Jane laughed. "Yes, I see you are. Well, a valentine is just a piece of poetry, with a picture to it, that anybody sends to a person on Valentine's Day."

"What's Valentine's Day?"

"Why, it's the day you send valentines, to be sure,--the 14th of February."

"Is it like Christmas? Was Valentine very good, and is it his birthday as Christmas is Christ's birthday?"

"Mercy, no! What queer things you do ask when you get going, Polly! Valentine's Day is just Valentine's Day, when folks send these poetry and picture things for fun, and don't sign their own names, only 'Your Valentine,' and that means somebody who has chosen--chosen to be your--well, your beau, maybe."

"What's a beau?" asked innocent Polly.

"Polly, you don't know **anything**!" cried Jane, in an exasperated tone. "A beau is--is somebody who likes you better 'n anybody else."

"Oh, I wish I had one!"

"Had one--what?" asked Jane.

"A beau to like me like that; to send me a valentine."

"Oh, oh! you are such a baby," laughed Jane.

"I ain't a baby!" cried Polly, indignantly; and then her lip quivered, and she began to cry.

"Hush, hush!" said Jane; "if Mrs. Banks hears you, she'll send you out of here quicker 'n a wink."

But Polly could not "hush" all at once, and continued to sob and sniff behind her apron; Jane trying in the mean time to soothe her, but not succeeding very well, until she thought to say,--

"If you won't cry any more, Polly, I'll get Martha"--Martha was the chamber-maid--"to show you *her* valentine; it's a beauty."

Polly dropped her apron and began to swallow her sobs, while Jane ran to Martha, who was very proud of her valentine, and very glad to show it even to little Polly Price; and the valentine *was* a beauty, as Jane had said. Polly, looking through the tears that still hung on her lashes at the group of little cherubs that were dancing out of lily-cups and roses, cried, "Angels, angels!" winding up with, "Oh, I *wish* somebody 'd send me a valentine!"

"She didn't know a thing about valentines; never heard of them till just now," Jane explained to Martha.

"Well, to be sure," said Martha, "she is the greenest little thing; but then she ain't never been to school like the rest of ye, and things is very quiet and out-of-the-way like in the Home here, and she's nothin' but a baby."

"I ain't a baby! I ain't, I ain't!" screamed Polly.

"Polly, Polly!" warned Jane. But Polly only burst out afresh in loud sobs and cries. Jane was a good-natured girl, but she could not stand this, and, reaching forward, she gave Polly a little shake, and said, "Now, Polly Price, you just stop and be a good girl, or I'll never have anything more to do with you."

Polly gasped. Three years ago, when she was first brought to the Home, she had been assigned to a little bed next the one that Jane occupied, and had been more or less under the elder girl's care. Jane had been very good to the child, and with her womanly ways and superior knowledge she stood to Polly for both mother and sister. No wonder, then, that she gasped at Jane's threat. What would she do if that threat were carried out, and Jane had nothing more to do with her? What would life be in the Home without Jane?

Polly did not ask herself these questions in exactly these words, but she felt the desolate possibility that had been suggested to her; and it was so appalling that it quite overpowered her flare of temper, and stopped her sobs and cries as effectually as Jane could have desired. But Jane herself, busy with her darning, did not notice the expression of Polly's face, and had no idea how deeply her words had penetrated the child's mind until hours afterwards, when, as she was preparing to go to bed, Polly's voice called softly,--

"Jane, haven't I been a good girl since?"

Jane started. "What in the world are you awake for now, Polly Price?" she asked. "It's nine o'clock. You ought to have been asleep long ago."

"I couldn't go to sleep, I felt so bad," answered Polly.

"You felt so bad; where? Have you got a sore throat?" inquired Jane, remembering that a good many of the children's illnesses began with sore throat.

"No, 'tisn't my throat."

"Where is it, then--your stomach?"

"No, it's--it's my feelin's. I felt bad 'cause--'cause you said if I didn't stop cryin' and be a good girl, you wouldn' ever have anythin' to do with me any more. But I did stop, and I **have** been a good girl since, haven't I?"

"Yes, oh, yes, you've been good since," bending down to tuck Polly in. As she stooped, Polly flung her arms around Jane's neck, and whispered,--

"Do you love me just the same, Jane?"

"Yes, I guess so," replied Jane, smiling.

"I love you better 'n anybody in the world, Jane."

"And you'd choose me to be your valentine, then, wouldn't you?" laughed Jane.

"Oh, yes, yes; and if I could only send you one of those po'try picture things, I'd send you the most bewt'f'lest I could find. Don't you wish I could, Jane?"

"Yes, of course I do."

"Did you ever have a valentine, Jane?"

"No, never."

"Those girls 'cross the street had 'em, and Martha had one. Why don't you and I have 'em, Jane?"

"You 'n' I? Those girls across the street know girls and boys who have fathers and mothers to give them money to buy valentines with."

"Why don't we know such girls and boys?"

"'Cause we don't. We're poor, and live in an Orphans' Home. Those girls only know folks that live like themselves."

"But Martha lives right here, just where we do, and Martha had a valentine."

"Martha's different. She's only paid for staying here to work. She's got folks outside that she belongs to. It was a cousin of hers sent her that valentine."

"Oh," and Polly gave a soft sigh, "I wish *we* had folks that we belonged to! Don't you, Jane?"

"*Don't* I!" and as Jane said this, she dropped down upon Polly's little bed, and covered her face with her hands.

"Oh, Jane, Janey! what's the matter? Has somebody hurted your feelings?"

"No, no," answered Jane, brokenly; "nobody in particular. I--I felt lonesome. I do sometimes when I get to thinking I don't belong to anybody and nobody belongs to me."

"Janey, *I* belongs to you, don't I?" And around Jane's neck two little arms pressed lovingly.

"You don't belong to me as a relation does. You ain't a sister or a cousin, you know."

"Can't you 'dopt me, Jane?"

Jane laughed through her tears. "What do you know about adopting?" she asked.

"Martha tole me 'bout it. She said folks of'n 'dopted children to be their very own, and that mebbe some time somebody'd 'dopt me; and I tole her then I didn' want anybody to 'dopt me, but--I'd like you to 'dopt me, Jane. Couldn't you?" with great earnestness.

"Of course not, Polly. Folks who adopt children are older 'n I am, and have money to take care of 'em. But I do wish some nice lady would adopt you,--some nice lady with a nice home."

"But I'd rather stay here 'long o' you, Jane. I don't want to go 'way from you; I'd be lonesome. But mebbe they'd 'dopt you too. Would you like to be 'dopted, Jane?"

"I don't know's I would. I'm too old now; I couldn't get to feel as if they were own folks, as if I really belonged to them, as you could. But, Polly," suddenly sitting up and looking very seriously at Polly, "you mustn't think I'm finding fault with the Home here. It's a very comfortable place, and we are treated well. I only feel kind of lonesome sometimes when I see girls like those across the street, who have mother-and-father homes."

"And valentines," cried Polly.

"Oh, Polly, Polly! you'll dream of valentines to-night," laughed Jane; "and mind you send me one in your dream, and the very prettiest you can find."

"I will, I will!" exclaimed Polly, flinging her arms again about Jane's neck, and giving her a good-night hug and kiss. "The very prettiest I can find! the very prettiest I can find!" And saying this over and over, Polly drifted away into the land of sleep.

CHAPTER II.

And sure enough, when it was well on towards morning, she did dream of valentines,--piles and piles of them, and out of them all she was hunting for the prettiest, when she heard a strangely familiar voice, calling,--

"Come, come, Polly! It's time to get up if you want any breakfast."

Polly opened her eyes to see Martha looking down at her. "Oh, Martha, Martha," she cried, "if you hadn't waked me, I should have got it. I'd **almost** found it, and in a little minute I'd 'a' had it sure."

"Had what?" asked Martha.

"Janey's valentine;" and, sitting up, Polly told her dream.

Martha laughed till the tears came. "You **are** the funniest young one we ever had here," was her comment, when she caught her breath. "Some time you'll dream you're an heiress, and wake up counting out your money to buy valentines with."

"What's an heiress?" inquired Polly.

"Oh, a girl that has a bankful of money," replied Martha, carelessly.

Polly gave one of her long-drawn "O--hs," then slipped out of bed, and began to dress so slowly that Martha said to her,--

"What are you dreaming about now, Polly?"

But Polly didn't answer. She was too busy pulling on her stockings, and thinking of something else that Martha had said, and this "something" was "a girl with a bankful of money." Martha little suspected what effect her words had had, little thought what a fine scheme she had set going. If she had, the scheme would certainly never have been carried out, or never have been carried out as Polly planned it. And Polly knew this perfectly well, and kept as still as a mouse all through breakfast,--so still that the matron, Mrs. Banks, asked, "Don't you feel well, Polly?"

whereat Polly choked over her oatmeal as she confusedly answered, "Yes, 'm."

If it had been any other child, Mrs. Banks would have suspected that there was some mischief brewing behind this stillness; but Polly had never been given to mischief, so she was not further questioned or observed, and thus left to herself she scampered back to the dormitory after the chamber-work was done, and, going straight to a small bureau that stood between Jane's bed and her own, she cautiously pulled out the lower drawer, and took from it a little toy house. This pretty toy house was nothing more nor less than a child's bank that had been given to Polly one Christmas, and into which she had dropped the pennies that had been bestowed upon her from time to time. Polly had long yearned for a paint-box; and whenever she went out, she used to stop at a certain shop-window where these tempting things were displayed, and wonder how much they cost. One day she summoned up courage to go in and ask the price of the smallest.

"Twenty-five cents," the clerk told her. Polly at first was dismayed. Twenty-five cents seemed a vast sum to her. But it was a long time yet to next Christmas, and perhaps by then she *might* find even as much as that in her bank. This hope had warmed her heart for weeks, so that when she was smarting under the first sense of disappointment about the valentines, she consoled herself with the thought of the little paint-box that might soon be hers. But when Martha had said, "Some time you'll dream you're an heiress, and wake up counting your money out," and had told her an heiress meant a girl with a bankful of money, like a flash of lightning came another thought into Polly's mind,--the thought that then and there from *her* little bank she might count the money to buy a valentine for her dear Jane; and once this thought had entered Polly's head there was no putting it out. Over and above everything it kept gaining, until it sent her to tugging at that red chimney. Then suddenly the chimney that had stuck so fast gave way.

Polly nearly fell backward, it was so sudden; but righting herself, she shook the treasure into her lap, and fell to counting it. She counted up to ten; that was as far as her knowledge of arithmetic went. Putting aside the ten pennies into a little pile, she began to count the rest. "One, two, three," she went on until--why, there was another pile of ten, and more yet; and the "more yet" counted up to five. Polly couldn't "do sums." She couldn't add these two piles of ten and the "more yet," and she couldn't ask Jane or any one else in the house to do it for her. But what she *could* do, what she *would* do, was to slip the whole treasure back into the bank, and take it around to the shop on the corner, the shop where she had seen the paint-boxes, and where she was sure she should also find plenty of valentines. So getting into her little coat and hood, she scampered out and off, unseen and unheard by any of the household. It was rather terrifying to find several other customers in the shop, but she had no time to wait until they had left, and, going bravely forward, she called out, "Please, I want a valentine." But the clerk was busy, and paid no attention to her; so she pressed a little nearer, and piped out again in a louder tone, "Please, I want a valentine."

But even this did not succeed in getting his attention. Oh, what *should* she do! Perhaps in another minute Jane or Martha or Mrs. Banks would have missed her, and be hunting for her; perhaps they would be sending a policeman after her. Oh dear! oh dear! And summoning up all her courage, she cried out in a voice full of sobs and tears, "Oh, please, *please*, I want a valentine right off now this minute!"

"Don't you see I'm busy now?" said the clerk, sharply.

But the lady he was waiting upon had turned and looked at Polly as she spoke, and immediately said to the clerk,--

"Oh, do attend to the child now. Her mother has probably told her to make haste."

"She hasn't any mother. She's one of the children at the Orphans' Home," replied the clerk in a lower tone.

"Oh!" And the lady started and looked at Polly with new interest, and then insisted still more earnestly that she should be attended to at once, at the same time beckoning Polly to come forward.

Polly obeyed her; but as she glanced at the cheap little five-cent valentines the clerk put before her, she shook her head disdainfully. "I want a bigger one; I want the bewt'f'lest there is," she informed him.

The young man laughed. "How much money have you got?" he asked.

Polly produced her bank, and triumphantly shook out its contents.

"Oh,"--laughing again,--"all that? How much is it?"

"I don't know jus' exac'ly. I can count up to ten, and there's two ten piles, and--and--five cents more."

"Oh, two tens and five. Yes, I see,"--running his fingers over the little heap,--

"that makes twenty-five. You've got twenty-five cents. Here are the twenty-five-cent valentines;" and he uncovered another box, and left her to make her choice.

"Twenty-five cents!" echoed Polly. Why, why, why, that was enough to buy the little paint-box! She glanced down at the twenty-five-cent valentines. They presented a dazzling sight of cherubs' heads and wings and flowery garlands. She lifted her chin a little higher, and there, staring her in the face, was the very little paint-box, with its two brushes and porcelain color plate, and it seemed to say to her: "Come, buy me now; come, buy me now. If you don't, somebody else will get me." And she *could* buy it now, if only--she gave up the valentine--Jane's valentine; and--why shouldn't she? She hadn't told Jane anything about it; Jane didn't expect it; Jane wouldn't ever know about it. Why shouldn't she? And Polly drew a deep sigh of perplexity as she asked herself this question.

"What is it?" a soft voice said to her here. "What is it that troubles you? Tell me. Perhaps I can help you."

Polly started, and turned to see the lady who had made way for her standing beside her. The lady smiled reassuringly as she met Polly's perplexed glance, and said again,--

"What is it? Tell me."

And Polly, looking up into the kind sweet face, told the whole story,--all about the long saving for the little paint-box, Jane's valentine, and everything, winding up eagerly with the appeal,--"And wouldn't *you* buy the paint-box now 'stead of the valentine, 'cos the paint-box mebbe'll be gone when I get more money?"

"Wouldn't I? Well, I don't know what I should have done when I was a little girl like you. I dare say, though, that I should have felt just as you do--have done just as you, I see, are going to do now."

"Bought the paint-box!" cried Polly.

"Yes, bought the paint-box," laughed the lady.

Polly beamed with smiles, and gave a rapturous look at the treasure that was so soon to be hers. But presently the rapture faded, and a new expression came into her face. The lady was watching her very attentively.

"Well, what now?" she inquired. "Doesn't the paint-box suit you?"

Polly gave an emphatic nod. Perhaps it was that nod that sent two little tears to her eyes.

"Then, if it suits you, shall I speak to the clerk, and tell him you've changed your mind about the valentine, and will buy the paint-box?"

Polly shook her head, and two more tears followed the first ones.

"You're not going to buy the paint-box?"

"N-o, I--I gu-ess not. I guess I'll buy the valentine. Jane didn't ever get a valentine, and she hasn't got anybody to give her one but me."

The blurring tears made Polly's eyes so dim here, she could scarcely see; but through the dimness she sent one last good-by look at the dear paint-box, and then resolutely turned to the valentines, from which she selected the biggest and "bewt'f'lest" she could find, the lady crowning her kindness by stamping and directing it, and finally mailing it in the letterbox just outside the shop door.

CHAPTER III.

"What yer watchin' for, Polly?"

Polly didn't answer.

"Guess I know," said Martha, laughing; "yer watchin' for the postman to bring yer a valentine."

"I ain't," said Polly.

Just then the postman crossed the street, and ring, ring, went the Home bell.

"I told you so," said Martha, as she ran down to answer it. In a minute she was back again holding out a big square envelope, and saying again, "I told you so."

"'T ain't for me," cried Polly.

"Ain't your name Polly Price?"

"Yes," faltered Polly.

"Well, here 's 'Polly Price' written as plain as print. Just look now!" and Martha held forth the missive.

Polly looked. She could read her own name in writing; and there it was, sure enough, plain as print,--Polly Price, and it was written on an envelope exactly like the one she had chosen to send to Jane. A fearful thought came into Polly's mind. She had told the lady her own name,--Polly Price,--and it was Polly Price she had written on the envelope instead of Jane McClane. Oh! oh! oh! and then Polly burst out,--

"It ain't mine, it ain't mine, it's Jane's. The lady made a mistake."

"What lady?"

"The lady in the shop."

"What shop?"

And then Polly had to tell the whole story.

"And that's where you were after breakfast, you little monkey, breaking a bank, and running away with it, to buy Jane McClane a valentine. Well, if this isn't the funniest thing I ever heard of. Jane! Jane! come up here and show Polly *your* valentine!" And up came Jane, her face beaming with smiles, holding in one hand a big square envelope, and in the other an open sheet all covered with lilies and roses and cherubs' faces; that very "bewt'f'lest valentine" that had been chosen for her.

Polly, staring at it in amazement, cried out, "Why, she's got it! she's got it!" And then, pulling open the envelope addressed to Polly Price, she stared in amazement again, and cried out, "Why, this is just like *that* one,--the one I bought for you, Janey!"

And then it was Jane's turn to cry out in amazement, to say, "*You* bought it; how did *you* buy it, Polly?"

"She broke a bank and ran away with the money," laughed Martha.

"I didn't, either. The chimney's made to come out, and the bank's my bank," retorted Polly, indignantly.

"You took *your* money,--your money you've been saving to buy the paint-box with, to buy this valentine for me?" asked Jane.

"Yes," faltered Polly.

"And gave up the paint-box! Oh, Polly, Polly, you're a dear;" and Jane swooped down upon Polly with a tremendous hug. Polly returned the embrace with ardor, and then, "Who d' you s'pose," she asked, "who d' you s'pose sent *me* one jus' exactly like yours? It must be somebody that likes me jus' as I like you, Janey."

"Mrs. Banks wants you to go down to the parlor, Polly. There's some one to see you," a voice interrupted here.

"To see *me*?" cried Polly.

"Yes,--don't stop to bother,--run along." And Polly ran along as fast as her feet could carry her, wondering as she went who had come to see *her*, who had never in her life had a visitor before. At the foot of the stairs she stopped in shy alarm. Then she tiptoed across the hallway to the parlor threshold, and there she saw the lady who had been so kind to her in the shop.

"Oh, it's you!" exclaimed Polly, joyfully.

The lady laughed, and held out her hand. "Yes, it's I," she said. "Did Jane get the valentine all right, and did she like it?"

Polly nodded, and then burst out with the story of her own valentine,--"Jus' like Janey's!"

"And who d' you s'pose sent it?" she asked confidingly, nestling against the lady's knee.

"I think it must have been one of the good Saint Valentine's messengers," answered the lady.

Polly's eyes opened very wide. "Saint Valentine! Tell me 'bout him," she said.

"A very wise man has told about him,--a man by the name of Wheatley,--and he says that this Valentine was a good bishop who lived long ago, and so famous for his love and charity that after he died he was called Saint Valentine, and a festival was held on his birthday, when all the people would send love tokens to their friends."

Polly's face was radiant. "Oh, I **thought** Valentine was a somebody very good, and that Valentine's Day was his birthday. I asked Jane if 't wasn't. Oh, Janey, Janey!" running to the foot of the stairs in her excitement, "come down and hear 'bout Saint Valentine!"

"Polly!" said Mrs. Banks, reprovingly.

"Oh, don't stop her," cried the lady. "I like to hear her, and I want to see Janey." After this there was nothing for Mrs. Banks to do but to send for Jane. As the strong, womanly-looking girl entered the room, a new idea entered the lady's mind. "It's the very thing," she said to herself,--"the very thing." At that instant carriage wheels were heard at the door, and the bell was rung sharply and impatiently. "Oh, it must be my Elise," said the lady.

The next instant the door was opened, and in hopped--that is the only word to use--a little lame girl of ten or eleven, lifting herself along by a crutch. She was very pale, and her eyes were sunken with suffering; but she looked about her with a smile, and said in a quick, lively way,--

"I got tired of driving 'round the square waiting for you, mamma; so I thought I'd come in."

"I'm glad you did; I wanted you to see--"

"I know--Polly! Mamma 's told me all about you, Polly, you and Jane and the valentine; and that's Jane. How do you do, Polly? how do you do, Jane?" nodding and laughing at them in a way that made Polly and Jane laugh too, whereupon this odd little girl exclaimed, "That's right, laugh, do! I like laughy folks;" and then, as she said this, her little figure swayed and would have fallen, if Jane, who was very quick of motion, hadn't sprung forward and caught her in her arms. The girl's face was all puckered up into little wrinkles of pain; but as soon as she could speak, she said, "Aren't you strong, though, Jane!"

Jane couldn't say a word, but Polly piped out, "If I let you have my valentine to look at a little while, do you think you'd feel better?"

"Lots, Polly, lots. Mamma told me about you; and when you come to stay with us, you'll be a regular treat."

"Stay with you?" cried Polly, wonderingly.

"Yes; what," turning to her mother, "haven't you asked her yet, mamma?"

"No; I've only talked with Mrs. Banks."

"Well, I'll talk to Polly. Polly, we've been looking for a nice little girl like you to come and stay at our house. I'm lame, and I can't do much. When mamma came home and told me about you and the bank and the paint-box and the valentine, I said, 'That's the girl for me; let's go and ask her to come.' And *won't* you come, Polly?"

"I--I'd like to if--if Jane can come too."

"Don't. Polly. I can't--I can't!" whispered Jane.

"Oh, mamma, mamma!" cried the lame Elise, entreatingly.

"Mamma" turned to Mrs. Banks. "If she *would* only come and help us,--come and try us, at least,--I'm sure we could make satisfactory arrangements."

Mrs. Banks nodded, and smiled approval. "Of course Jane can go if she chooses."

"And you *will* choose,--you will, won't you, Jane?"

"Course she will," cried Polly; and then everybody laughed, and everything was as good as settled from that moment. Then it was that Polly burst out, "I should be puffickly happy now if I only knew jus' who that mess'nger was that sent my valentine."

"Tell her, mamma, tell her!" called out Elise; and "mamma" bent down, and said to Polly,--

"It was somebody who saw what a loving heart a certain little girl had when she chose to give up her paint-box to buy her dear Jane a valentine."

"'Twas you, 'twas you!" cried Polly, joyfully. "Oh, I jus' love Valentine's Day, and I knew it must be Somebody's birfday,--some very good Somebody!"

SIBYL'S SLIPPER.
CHAPTER I.

When Sir William Howe succeeded General Gage as governor and military commander of the New England province, he at once set to work to make himself and the King's cause popular in a social way by giving a series of fine entertainments in the stately Province House.

To these entertainments were bidden all the Boston townsfolk who were loyal to the British crown. Amongst such, none were more prominent or made more welcome than Mr. Jeffrey Merridew and his pretty young niece, Sibyl.

Mr. Merridew was a stanch royalist, though he was by no means a violent hater of the rebels. Many of them were his old friends and neighbors; and his only brother, Dr. Ephraim Merridew,--Sibyl's father,--was a rebel at heart, though in far-away Barbadoes, where he was at that time engaged in business, he could not serve the rebel cause in person, as he would gladly have done. But he left behind him a son who, in full sympathy with his father's views, ranged himself boldly on the rebel side, as part and parcel of the American army.

A rebel relative in Barbadoes was not a matter to trouble oneself about greatly, but a rebel relative on the spot, so to speak,--for young Ephraim was only four miles away at the Cambridge rallying-ground,--was a different thing; and, amiable and easy-going as Mr. Jeffrey Merridew was disposed to be, his nephew's close proximity could not, under the peculiar circumstances, but be embarrassing and disturbing on occasions; for the young man, besides being his nephew, was Sibyl's brother, and Sibyl, as a member of a royalist's family,--for her father on his departure for Barbadoes had left his motherless girl in her uncle's charge,--could not, of course, be allowed free intercourse with one who had placed himself in an attitude of active hostility to the royal cause.

When Sibyl was apprised of this dictum, she at once made passionate protest against it. "What harm do the King's soldiers think poor Eph can do them by now and then paying a visit to his sister?" she asked her uncle scornfully.

"Harm? You are very young, Sibyl, and don't understand these things. Your brother has chosen very foolishly to join the rebel forces, and so has made himself one of our acknowledged enemies; and I never heard of declared enemies in time of war walking in and out of each other's houses like tame cats," answered Mr. Merridew, sarcastically.

"But Eph, such a boy as Eph, only nineteen, only two years older than I! What harm could he do now, more than he has ever done, by coming to his uncle's house as a visitor?" still persisted Sibyl, rather foolishly.

"What harm!" exclaimed Mr. Merridew, impatiently. "What a child you are, Sibyl! Why, his coming here would compromise me fatally with the royal government. I should be suspected of disloyalty, and do you think that he, your brother, could be in any such communication with us and fail to see and hear many things that might bring us disaster if reported to his officers?"

"You think Eph would be so mean as to tell tales?" exclaimed Sibyl, in high indignation.

"Tell tales!" repeated Mr. Merridew, flinging back his head with irrepressible laughter at Sibyl's ignorance. Why, my dear, the reporting of important facts, however gained in times of war, is part of war tactics; it is not called 'telling tales.'"

"And would you--would you, if you were in Ephraim's camp as a visitor,-- would you--"

"Tell tales?" laughed Mr. Merridew. "Indeed I would, if I heard anything worth telling,--anything that I thought would save the cause I believed to be a righteous cause." Then, more seriously: "Why, Sibyl, it would be my duty to do it."

"Oh! oh!" cried Sibyl, "it is odious, odious, all this war business."

"Yes, I grant you that; but who is to blame for bringing this odious business upon us? Who but these foolish malcontents, these rebels, like--"

"Like my father and my brother," broke in Sibyl, hotly, as Mr. Merridew hesitated.

"Yes, like your father and your brother, I am sorry to say," concluded her uncle, gravely.

"No, no, no!" cried Sibyl, excitedly. "It is not they who are to blame. They are good and brave and wise. They only want justice and fair play. It is the King's folk who are to blame,--the King's folk who want to oppress the people with unjust taxes, that they may live in greater grandeur."

Mr. Merridew stared in silent astonishment at this unexpected outburst. Then, in a severer tone than his niece had ever heard from his lips, he said,--

"So this is the treasonable talk you have heard from your brother; these are the teachings that he has been instilling into you? Ah, it is none too soon that you are cut off from the influence of that headstrong boy."

"But it was my father who instilled these teachings into my brother. They are his principles, and they are my principles too!"

"Your principles!" and Mr. Merridew, his sense of humor immensely tickled at the sound of this fine word, that rolled off with such an assumption of dignity from those rosy young lips, burst into a great laugh. Yet then and there he said to himself, "That Jackanapes of a boy, to fill her head with this treasonable stuff! But we'll see, we'll see if we can't crowd all such stuff out with livelier things when we have those fine doings at the Province House Sir William is talking of. Her principles! The little parrot!" and he laughed again.

CHAPTER II.

"And you're to dance the last dance with me, remember, Miss Merridew."

"Indeed, Sir Harry, I will not promise you that."

"You will not promise? But you *have* promised."

"*Have* promised? What do you mean, sir? I think you are forgetting yourself!" and Miss Sibyl Merridew lifted up her graceful head with a little air of hauteur that was by no means unbecoming to her piquant beauty.

But young Sir Harry Willing was not to be put down by this pretty little provincial,--not he; and so, lifting up *his* head with an air of hauteur, he said to Miss Sibyl,--

"I crave Miss Merridew's pardon, but perhaps if she will reflect a moment she will recall what she said to me yester morning when I begged her to give me the pleasure of dancing the last minuet with her to-night."

Waving her great plumy feather fan to and fro, Sibyl looked across it at her companion, and answered in a little sweetly impertinent tone,--

"But I never reflect."

"So I should judge, madam," retorted the youth, wrathfully; "but perhaps," he went on, "if Miss Merridew will deign to bestow a glance upon this"--and the young fellow pulled from his pocket a gold-mounted card and letter case, out of which he took a tablet upon which was written: "Met Miss Sibyl Merridew this morning on the mall. She promised to dance the last minuet with me to-morrow night. Mem. Send roses if they are to be had in the town!"

Sibyl blushed as she read this. Then lifting the flowers--Sir Harry's roses--to her face for a moment, she dropped a demure courtesy and said, with a gleam of fun in her eyes,--

"If Sir Harry finds that it is necessary for *him* to recall his friends and engagements by memorandum notes, he certainly cannot expect an untutored provincial maid, who carries no such orderly appliance about with her, to charge *her* mind unaided."

"An untutored provincial maid!" exclaimed Sir Harry, all his wrath extinguished by her pretty recognition of his flowers and his admiration of her ready wit,--"an untutored provincial maid! By my faith, Miss Sibyl, you'd put to shame many a court dame. But, hark, what's that? As I live, the musicians are tuning up for the minuet." And smilingly he held out his hand to her.

"A very pretty pair," said more than one of the assembled company, as the two took their places in the beautifully decorated ball-room; and as the dance progressed, Mr. Jeffrey Merridew, watching his niece from his post of observation, said to himself with, a congratulatory smile,--

"Where now are Miss Sibyl's fine rebel principles? I scarcely think they would stand a test."

Almost at that very moment Sir Harry, boy as he was, spite of his one-and-twenty years, was giving vent to a little boastful talk about "our army" and "those undisciplined rebels who would never stand the test against a full regiment of regulars."

"Why," Sir Harry declared at length, led on by Sibyl's air of great interest, "we have positive information that their troops at Cambridge have neither arms nor ammunition to carry on a defence, and they are in a sorry condition every way; it is impossible for them to resist us successfully. We shall literally sweep them off the face of the earth if they attempt it."

"And you--the King's troops?" inquired Sibyl.

"We--well, we have been a little straitened ourselves for the munitions of war," replied the young aide-de-camp, "but by to-morrow night a vessel will arrive for us that will relieve all such necessities. Ah," with a gay smile, "what would not these rebels give to get possession of this information, and put their cruisers on the alert to capture such a prize!"

"But there is no possibility of this?"

"Not the slightest. But you are pale,--don't be alarmed; there is no danger. The rebels have no suspicion of the expected arrival, we are certain."

"But if they had?"

"Well, that might alter the case. Their seamen know their business better than their landsmen."

All this in the pauses of the dance. When they started up again, the music had accelerated its time, and down the great hall they led the way at a fine pace; but in swinging about to return, Sir Harry felt his companion falter.

"What is it?" he asked anxiously.

"My slipper," she replied with a vexed laugh; and, stooping as she spoke, she whisked off a little satin shoe, the high hollow metal heel of which had suddenly given way. Certainly no more dancing that night. For that matter, though, it was near the end of the ball. But could not *he* do something? Sir Harry asked. He had tinkered gunscrews; why not a slipper? No, no; nothing could be done then and there. A new heel must be hammered and fitted on.

But then and there Sibyl had a sudden inspiration. ***Something could*** be done. She was to go to Madame Boutineau's rout the next evening. She needed these very slippers for that occasion. Would Sir Harry--on his way to his quarters that night-

-would he think it beneath his dignity to leave the slippers at Anthony Styles the shoemaker's? It was just there by the tavern at the sign of the gilded boot. He had only to drop the shoe, with a message she would write to go with it, into the tunnel-box by the door, and Anthony would find it by daylight and set to work upon it at once, that she might not be disappointed, for it was a longish job, she knew.

Beneath his dignity! Sir Harry laughed. He was only too glad to do her bidding.

And would he then give her a bit of paper and pencil and take her to the cloak-room for a moment?

Alone in the cloak-room, Sibyl wrote her message to Anthony Styles. Folding the paper in the slipper, and wrapping the whole in her pocket-handkerchief, she fastened the parcel securely with the silken cord that had held her fan.

"And may I have the last dance to-morrow night?" asked Sir Harry, smilingly, as he took leave of her a few minutes later.

"Perhaps, if I may depend upon you--and Anthony Styles," she answered. Her eyes sparkled like dark jewels as she spoke; her cheeks burned like red twin roses.

CHAPTER III.

Robe of satin and Brussels lace,
　　Knots of flowers and ribbons too,
　　Scattered about in every place,
　　For the revel is through.

And there, in the midst of all this pretty disorder of satin and lace and flowers, sits Sibyl, far into the night, or rather morning, turning over and over in her mind something that effectually banishes sleep.

By and by, as she turns it over for the twentieth time, she says aloud to herself: "To think that it should be given to *me* to do,--made *my* duty! Uncle Jeffrey taught me that, as he has taught me many things these past months,--to keep my own counsel, for one thing.

"Ah, Uncle Jeffrey, you have fancied me all these months naught but a vain little puppet who could be led to forget anything in a round of routs and balls. Well, I like the routs and balls dearly, dearly, but I like something else better. I like what my father has taught us, what my dear Eph is going to fight for, and perhaps die for, far, far better. Yet I felt like a cheat to-night as I led Sir Harry on to tell me what he did,--Sir Harry, who thinks me, as all the rest do, a stanch little Tory, for I have kept my counsel indeed, and no one suspects. But oh, it is odious, it is odious, this war business; yet I have been taught how to do my duty, and I have done it. Yes, I have done my duty, for 'the reporting of important facts, however gained, in times of war, is part of war tactics.' Yes, these are your words, Uncle Jeffrey, and oh, how they flashed up to me to-night when Sir Harry told me of the British vessel, and how they fairly rung in my ears like an order, when it suddenly came to me how I could get this important fact that I had gained sent to the right quarter by means of good Anthony Styles and that parcel-box of his, through which so many messages have gone safely.

"Oh, I could laugh, I could laugh, if I didn't shiver so, when I think of it! Sir Harry, Sir Harry of all persons, dropping that message into Anthony Styles's hands,--Anthony Styles, the stanch rebel whom they think a stanch Tory! Oh, I could laugh, I could laugh! And now if everything goes well,--if everything goes well, my dear rebels will not be swept off the earth by British arms quite yet!

"But, hark! that is the clock; it is striking one, and I out of bed and gabbling to myself in this foolish way of mine, 'like a play-acting woman,' as Uncle Jeffrey would say of me. But I will not stay up a minute longer. So good-night, good-night, my dear rebels, g--ood-night!"

    *   *   *   *   *

The clock was striking four the next afternoon when a weather-beaten man, who had a look as if he had once been a seaman, knocked at the side door of Mr. Jeffrey Merridew's mansion and asked to see young Mistress Merridew.

"It's Shoemaker Styles," the maid informed Sibyl, "and he says you must come down and try on the slipper he has brought; he's not sure about the heel. He's in the hall-room, mem."

It was with a wildly beating heart that Sibyl, obeying this summons, ran down to the little hall-room where Anthony Styles awaited her.

He stood with the slipper in his hand as she entered the room; and before he could close the door behind her, he called out in a frank, loud voice: "I thought you had better try on the shoe, miss; I wasn't sure of the heel."

The moment the door was closed, however, he came forward eagerly, and in a low tone said: "It's all right, little mistress. I heard the click of the tunnel-box last night, for I hadn't turned in, and afore many minutes I was up and off in my boat with the message in my head; I burnt the paper! There was a stiff breeze, and I reached the cutter in the quickest time I ever made, and got back afore daylight with nobody the wiser. Shoemaker Styles understands his old sailor business better than shoemaking," with a grim laugh, "and no Tory knows these waters as I do."

"And it's all right, and the end will be all right?" faltered Sibyl, anxiously.

"All right! You'll know for yourself by nightfall, perhaps; and now God bless you, little mistress. You've done a great service; and if ever Anthony Styles can sarve you, he'll do it with a whole heart,--God bless you, God bless you!" and with these words Shoemaker Styles hurried off, leaving Sibyl with the slipper still in her hand, and both of them quite oblivious of that important trying-on process.

The day after the ball was a busy one for Sir Harry Willing, and it was not until late in the afternoon that he felt himself at liberty to take his accustomed saunter about town.

As he came in sight of the gilded boot, he smilingly thought: "I wonder if Shoemaker Styles has done his duty by the little slipper; if he has, I shall dance with my lady Sibyl at Madame Boutineau's this evening."

But Sir Harry did not dance at Madame Boutineau's that evening, for when at nightfall he returned to his quarters, he was met by the disastrous tidings that the long-looked for, eagerly expected British brig, loaded with supplies for the King's army, had been captured off Lechmere's Point by the Yankee rebels.

It was not many months after this capture that the British evacuated Boston. When Sir Harry Willing took leave of Sibyl Merridew, he pleaded for some token of remembrance.

"You will not promise yourself to me," he said in reproachful accents, "but give me some token of yourself, some gage of amity at least."

"But what--what can I give you, Sir Harry?" asked Sibyl, not a little touched and troubled.

"Give me the little slipper you wore that night we danced together at the Province House."

"That--that slipper?" and Sibyl blushed and paled.

"Yes--ah, you will, you will."

A moment's hesitation; then with a strange smile, half grave, half gay, Sibyl answered, "I will."

A LITTLE BOARDING-SCHOOL SAMARITAN.
CHAPTER I.

It was Saturday afternoon, and Eva Nelson and Alice King were sitting in their little study parlor at the Hill House Seminary poring over their lesson chapter for the next day. It was the tenth chapter of St. Luke, with the story of the good Samaritan. At last Eva flung herself back and exclaimed, "We *can't* be good as they were in those Bible days, no matter *what* anybody says; things are different."

"Of course they are," responded Alice. "Who said they weren't?"

Eva turned to the volume before her, and read aloud about the man who had fallen among thieves, and the good Samaritan who came along and bound up his wounds and took care of him.

"Now how can we do things like that?" she said.

"Oh, Eva, I should think you were about five or six years old instead of a girl of thirteen. Nobody means that you are to do just those particular things. What they do mean now is that you are to be good to people who are in trouble,--people who need things done for them."

"Well, I'd be good to them if I had a chance; but what chance do I have now with all my lessons? When I grow up, I shall belong to charitable societies, as mamma does, and give things to poor folks, and go to see them. I can't now; girls of our age can't, of course."

"We can do some things in vacations,--get up fairs and things of that kind, and give the money to the poor."

"Oh, I've done that. I helped in a fair last summer, and we gave the money to the children's hospital. But Miss Vincent said last week that all of us could find ways of doing good every day if we would keep our eyes and ears and hearts open; and I've felt ever since that she was keeping her eyes open on the watch for something she expected *me* to do."

"Nonsense! She knows as well as we do that we haven't time to do any more now. She means when we grow older. But look at the clock,--five minutes to sup-per-time, and I've got to 'do' my hair all over, the braid is so frowzely."

"What makes you braid it? Why don't you let it hang in a curl, as you used to?"

"I told you why yesterday,--because that Burr girl has made me sick of curls, with that great black flop of hers stringing down her back. She'd make me sick of anything. I haven't worn my red blouse since she came out with that fiery thing of hers. *Isn't* it horrid?"

"Yes, horrid!"

A few minutes after, as Eva and Alice were stirring their cocoa at the supper-table, the girl they had been criticising came hastily into the dining-room and took her place. She was a tall girl for her age, with a heavy ungainly figure, a swarthy skin, and black hair which was tied back in a long curl. She wore a dark plaid skirt, with a blouse of fiery red cashmere, and a hair ribbon of a deep violet shade. Nothing could have been more ill-matched or more unbecoming. The girl who sat beside her, pretty Janey Miller, was a great contrast, with her blond curls, her rosy cheeks, and simple well-fitting dress of blue serge. Her every movement, too, was as full of grace as Cordelia Burr's was exactly the reverse. Everything seemed to go well with Janey; everything seemed to go ill with Cordelia. She spilled her cocoa, she dropped her knife, she crumbled her gingerbread, and she clattered her cup and saucer. Certainly she was not a very pleasant person to sit near. But Janey tried to conceal her annoyance, and succeeded very well, until at the end of the meal Cordelia, in her headlong haste in leaving her seat, tipped over a glass of water upon her neighbor's pretty blue dress. This was too much, for Janey, and it was little wonder that she jumped up with an impatient exclamation, nor that she declared to Eva and Alice a little later that Cordelia ought to be ashamed of herself for being so careless, and that she did wish she didn't have to sit next to her.

"I suppose, though, I shall have to sit there until the end of this term; but there's *one* thing I'm not going to do any more,--I'm not going to dance with her. She doesn't keep step, and she *does* dress so!" concluded Janey.

"Yes, she does dress dreadfully; and to think it's her own fault. She chooses her things herself," said Eva.

"No!" exclaimed Janey.

"Yes, she does; her mother is 'way off somewhere, and Cordelia gets what she likes."

"And she doesn't know any better than to like such horrid things! Sometimes she looks as if she'd lived with wild Indians!"

"That's it; that's it, I forgot!" shouted Eva. "She *has* lived 'way off out in a Territory on an Indian reservation. Her father is an army officer of some kind."

"Young ladies, young ladies, look at your clocks!" suddenly called a voice outside the door.

"Why, goodness, it's bedtime!" whispered Janey. "Good-night, good-night."

The next afternoon, when the Sunday classes were in session in the great hall, Janey, who was not in the same class with Eva and Alice, wondered as she looked across at them what they could be talking about that seemed so interesting. This is what they were talking about: Alice, in her clever exact way, had told Miss Vincent the whole of that little Saturday-night talk concerning the good Samaritan. Miss Vincent smiled when Alice told of Eva's odd simplicity of application; but as Alice went on and presented Eva's perplexity and her plea for girls of her age,--their lack of time and all that, and her own assurance to Eva that Miss Vincent did not mean what Eva fancied that she did,--Miss Vincent, in a quick, decided, almost eager way, started forward and cried,--

"Oh, but I did! I did mean it. Girls of your age can do--oh, so much! You are thinking of only one way of doing,--helping the poor, visiting people in need. I *don't* think you can do much of that. I think that *is* mostly for older people; but you live in a little world of your own,--a girls' world, where you can help or hurt one another every day and hour by what you do or say. Oh, I know, I know, for I went through such suffering once,--was so hurt when I might have been helped. But let me tell you about it, and then you'll see what I mean. It was when I was between twelve and thirteen. We had just come to Boston, and I was sent to a strange school. I was very shy, but ashamed to show that I was. So when the girls stared at me, as girls will, and giggled amongst themselves about anything, I thought they were staring in an unfriendly way and laughing at *me*, and I immediately straightened up and put on a stiff and what I tried to make an indifferent manner. This only prejudiced them against me, and the unfriendliness I had fancied became very soon a reality, and I was snubbed or avoided in the most decided way. I tried to bear this silently, to act as if I didn't care for a while, but I became so lonely at length I thought I would try to conciliate them. I dare say, however, my shy manner was still misunderstood, for I was not encouraged to go on. What I suffered at this time I have never forgotten. The girls were no worse than other girls, but they had started out on a wrong track, and gradually the whole flock of them, one led on by what another would say or do, were down upon me. It was a sort of contagious excitement, and they didn't stop to think it might be unjust or cruel. Things went on from bad to worse, until at last I gave up trying to conciliate, and turned on them like a little wild-cat. I forgot my timidity,--forgot everything but my desire to be even with them, as I expressed it. But it wasn't an even conflict,--thirty girls against one; and at length I did something dreadful. I was going from the school-room to a recitation room with my ink-bottle; that I had been to have filled, when I met in the hall three of 'my enemies,' as I called them. In trying to avoid them I ran against them. They thought I did it purposely, and at once accused me of that, and other sins I happened to be innocent of, in a way that exasperated me. I tried to go on, but they barred my progress; and then it was that I lost all control of myself, and in a sort of frantic fury flung the ink-bottle that I held straight before me. I could never recall the details of anything after that. I only remember the screams, the opening of doors, the teachers hastening up, a voice saying, 'No; only the dresses are injured; but she might have killed somebody!' In the answers to their questions the teachers got at something of the truth, not all of it. They were very much shocked at a state of things they had not even suspected; but my violence prejudiced them against me, as was natural, and they had little sympathy for me. Of course I couldn't remain at the school after that. I was not expelled. My father took me away, yet I always felt that I went in disgrace."

"They were horrid girls,--horrid!" cried Alice, vehemently.

"No; they were like any ordinary girls who ***don't think***. But you see how different everything might have been if only *one* of them had thought to say a kind word to me; had seen that I might have been suffering, and"--smiling down upon Eva--"been a good Samaritan to me."

"They were horrid, or they **would** have thought," insisted Alice. "I'm sure *I* don't know any girls who would have been so stupid."

"Nor I, nor I," chimed in two or three other voices. But Eva Nelson was silent.

CHAPTER II.

"You are the most ridiculous girl for getting fancies into your head, Eva; and you never get things right,--never!"

"I think you are very unkind."

"Well, you can think so. *I* think--"

"Hush!" in a warning voice; "there's some one knocking at the door;" then, louder, "Come in;" and responsive to this invitation, Janey Miller entered.

"What were you and Eva squabbling about?" she asked, looking at Alice.

"Cordelia Burr!" replied Alice, disdainfully.

"Cordelia Burr?"

"Yes. What do you think? Eva wants to take her up and be intimate with her."

"Now, Alice, I don't," cried Eva. "I only wanted to be kinder to her. When Miss Vincent told us that story yesterday, I couldn't help thinking of Cordelia, and that we might be on the wrong track with **her**, as those horrid girls were with Miss Vincent."

"'Those horrid girls'! What does she mean, Alice?" asked Janey.

Alice repeated Miss Vincent's story. "And Eva," she went on, "has got it into her head that Cordelia is like what Miss Vincent was, and that we are like those horrid girls."

"Not like them; not as bad as they were, **yet**; but we might be if we kept on, maybe."

"But it isn't the same thing at all, Eva," struck in Janey. "That sweet, pretty Miss Vincent could never have been anything like Cordelia; and we--I'm sure none of us have been like those horrid girls. I don't like Cordelia, but I don't say anything hateful to her, and none of us girls do."

"But you--we don't want her 'round with us, and we show it. We won't dance with her if we can help it, and we've managed to keep her out of things that we were in, a good many times."

"Well, nobody wants a person 'round with them who makes herself so disagreeable as Cordelia does; and as for dancing with her, she's never in step, and is always treading upon you and bumping against you; and in everything else it's just the same."

"Maybe she's shy, as Miss Vincent was."

"Shy! Cordelia Burr shy!" shouted Alice, in derision.

"No; she's anything but shy," said Janey; "she's as uppish and independent as she can be."

"But maybe she puts that on. Maybe--"

"Maybe she's a princess in disguise!" cried Alice, scornfully.

"Well, I don't care. I think we ought to try and see if perhaps we are not on the wrong track with her; and I--"

"Now, Eva," and Alice looked up very determinedly, "if you begin to take notice of Cordelia, there'll be no getting away from her; she'll be pushing herself in where she isn't wanted, constantly. And there's just one thing more: I'll say, if you *do* begin this, you'll have to do it alone. I won't have anything to do with it; and, you'll see, the rest of the girls won't; and you'll be left to yourself with Miss Cordelia, and a nice time you'll have of it."

Eva made no answer. Indeed, she would have found it hard to speak, for she was choking with tears,--tears that presently found vent in "a good cry," as Alice and Janey left the room.

What should she do? What *could* she do with all the girls against her? If she could only tell Miss Vincent, she could advise her. But Miss Vincent had been summoned home by illness that very morning.

Poor Eva! the way before her looked extremely difficult. She was very sensitive, and Miss Vincent's story had made an impression upon her that could not be got rid of. She was astonished to find it had not made the same impression upon Alice,--that Alice had not seen in it, as she had, a clear direction what to do, or what to try to do; and now here was Janey, as entirely out of sympathy, and Alice had said that all the rest of the girls would be the same. If Alice was right, it might-

-it might make a bad matter worse; it might make the girls dislike Cordelia more, to--to interfere. For a moment Eva felt that this view of the matter would solve her difficulty, by exonerating her from undertaking her task. The next moment there flashed into her mind these words of Miss Vincent's: "If only one of them had thought to say a kind word to me."

About half an hour later Alice and Janey, with three or four of the other girls, were practising in the gymnasium together.

"I wonder where Eva is?" whispered Alice. "She's always here at this time; she is so fond of the gym."

"She didn't like what we said, so perhaps she won't come to-day," whispered Janey.

"Well, I had to say what I did; if I hadn't, Eva would have--But there she is now," as the door opened. Then aloud, "Eva, Eva, come over here and try the bars with us."

Eva 's heart gave a little jump of gladness as she accepted this pleasantly spoken invitation. She hated to be on ill terms with anybody, and especially with Alice, of whom she was fond; and as she went forward and swung herself lightly up beside her, she forgot for the moment everything that was unpleasant.

There was a pretty little running exercise up and down a gently inclined plane that was in great favor at the school; and when the three swung down from the bars, Alice proposed that they should try the race-track, as they called it.

They were just starting off when the door opened, and Cordelia Burr came in. She stared about her in her odd frowning way, and then hurried forward to join the runners. Eva gave a little start of recoil. Alice gave more than a start. She seized Eva and Janey by the wrists, and, pushing them before her, sent a nod and backward to several others who had left the bars to come over to the race-track. She did not say even to herself that she meant to crowd Cordelia out; but the fact was accomplished, nevertheless, for by the time Cordelia reached the track there was no room for her. Eva had seen this same kind of stratagem enacted before, and thought it "fun." Now, with her eyes and ears and heart open, through Miss Vincent's influence, the fun took on a different aspect. But what--what ought she to do? What *could* she do then? She might slip out and offer her place to Cordelia. But the girls, and Alice-- Alice specially--would be *so* angry. Oh, no, no, she couldn't; it wouldn't do to brave them like that! Looking up as she came to this conclusion, she saw Cordelia stand-ing all alone, her face flushed with anger or mortification, perhaps both.

"If only one of them had thought to say a kind word to me!" flashed again through Eva's mind.

"Go on, go on; what are you lagging for?" whispered Alice, as Eva's pace fal-tered here.

Eva's eyes were fixed upon Cordelia, who had crossed the room and was going towards the door.

"Go on, go on; you are stopping us all!" exclaimed Alice, impatiently.

But with a sudden supreme effort Eva flung away her cowardice, and dashed off the track, crying, "Cordelia! Cordelia!"

Cordelia turned her head a moment, yet without staying her steps.

Eva sprang forward and put out her hand, crying again, "Cordelia! Cordelia!"

The runners had all stopped with one accord, as Eva sprang forward. What was it, what was she going to do, to say, to Cordelia? Even Alice and Janey, who knew more than the others what was in Eva's mind,--even they wondered what she was going to do, to say. And when in the next instant she cried breathlessly, "We--I--didn't mean to crowd you out; it--it wasn't fair; and--and you'll come back and take my place, Cordelia, won't you?" they, even Alice and Janey, forgot to be angry; forgot everything at the moment in their astonishment and an involuntary admiration for Eva's courage in daring to do as she did--***against them all***! What Alice might have said or done when that moment had gone, and her mortification at Eva's disregard of her opinion had had chance to start afresh, it is impossible to tell, for before that could take place something very unexpected happened, and this was a most unlooked-for action on Cordelia's part. They all looked to see her turn with one of her haughty, or what Alice and Janey called her uppish, independent glances upon Eva, and reject at once her appeal and offer. Instead of that--instead of coldness and haughty independence--they saw her, they heard her, suddenly give a shuddering, sobbing sigh, and then, dropping her face into her hands, break down utterly in a paroxysm of tears,--not tears of anger, of violence of any kind, but tears that, like the shuddering, sobbing sigh, seemed to come from a sore heart after long repression.

"Oh, Cordelia! Cordelia!" burst out Eva, putting her arm about Cordelia, "don't, don't cry."

Cordelia could not respond to this appeal, could not stop her tears; but as Eva bent over her in tender pity, she leaned forward and rested her head against the arm that encircled her. As the girls who stood watching saw this, as they saw Eva with her own pocket-handkerchief try to wipe away those tears, as they heard her say again, "Oh, Cordelia! Cordelia! don't, don't cry!" they looked at one another in a confused, questioning sort of way; and then, as they heard Eva speak again and with a breaking voice, as they saw the bright drops of sympathy and pity and regret gather in her eyes and roll down her cheeks, they started uneasily, and one and then another moved forward in a half-frightened, embarrassed fashion towards the door. Eva glanced up at them reproachfully as they passed. Were they not going to say a word, not a single word, to Cordelia? Hadn't they any pity for her; hadn't they any shame for what they had done? Goaded by these thoughts, she burst out passionately, "Oh, girls, I should think--" and then broke down completely, and bowed her head against Cordelia's, unable to say another word. But somebody else took up her words,--the very words she had used a second ago,--somebody else whispered,--

"Don't cry, don't cry." At the same moment a hand touched her shoulder, and she looked up to see--Alice King standing beside her. And then it seemed as if all the others were anxious to press forward; and one of them, the youngest of all, little Mary Leslie, a girl of ten, suddenly piped out,--

"We--we didn't know as you'd care, like this, Cordelia."

And then Cordelia lifted up her swollen tear-stained face, and faltered out: "Care? How--how could I hel--help caring?"

"But we thought--we thought you didn't like us," said another, hesitatingly.

"And I--I thought you hated and despised me, and I thought you'd despise me more if--if I showed that I cared!" and Cordelia gave another little sob, and covered her poor disfigured face again.

"Oh, Cordelia, Cordelia!" cried one and then another, pityingly; and then a voice, it sounded like Alice's, said, "We've been on the wrong track."

Just here a bell in the hall--the signal to those in the gymnasium that their half-hour was up--rang sharply out, and ashamed and sorry and repentant the girls hurried away to their rooms to change their dresses and prepare for dinner.

"Oh, Alice, Alice, you were so good!" cried Eva, flinging her arms around Alice's neck the moment they were alone together.

"Good? Don't--don't say that," exclaimed Alice, starting back.

"But you *were*. I--I was so afraid you'd be angry with me. I--"

Alice now flung *her* arms around her friend, and gave her a little hug, as she cried: "Oh, Eva, it's you who've been good. I--I've been--a little fiend, I suppose, and I *was* horridly angry at first; but when I--I saw how--that Cordelia really was--that she really felt what she did, I--oh, Eva!" laughing a little hysterically, "when you stood mopping up Cordelia's tears, all I could think was, *there's* a little Samaritan."

"Oh, Alice!"

"I did truly, and you'll go on as good as you've begun, and end by liking and loving Cordelia because you pity her, I dare say. But though I'm going to behave myself, and *bear* with her, I shall never come up to that, for she is so queer and so clumsy, and she *does* dress so! I'm going to behave myself, though, I am,--I am; but I hope she won't expect too much, that she won't push forward too fast now."

"Oh, Alice, I don't believe Cordelia's that kind of a girl at all; she's too proud. I think she's awkward and queer, and don't know about dress and things, because she's lived 'way out there on the plains, but she'll improve when she finds we mean to be friendly to her; you see if she doesn't."

And Eva was right. By the end of the term Cordelia had improved so much in the friendlier atmosphere that surrounded her that she was quite like another girl. No longer uneasy and suspicious, she lost her self-consciousness, and with it a good deal of her awkwardness and apparent ill temper, and began to blossom out happily and cheerily as a girl should. Even her face brightened and bloomed in this atmosphere, and by and by she took Eva and Alice and Janey into her confidence so far that she shyly asked their advice about her dress, and profited by it to such an extent that Alice could no longer say, "She *does* dress so!"

ESTHER BODN.
CHAPTER I.

"Oh, Laura, I want you to come home with me to-morrow after school and dine, and stay the evening. We shall be alone together, for mamma and papa are going out to a dinner-party. You'll come, won't you? Mamma told me to ask you."

"If it was any other evening."

"Now, Laura, you are not going to say you can't come!"

"I must, Kitty. I have promised to take tea with Esther Bodn."

"Esther Bodn!"

"Yes, she asked me to fix a day this week when I could come, and I fixed Thursday,--to-morrow."

"But, Laura, can't you postpone it? Tell her how it is,--that mamma and papa are going away, and that Mary and Agnes are in New York, and I shall be all alone unless you come. Can't you do that, Laura?"

"I don't want to do that, Kitty."

"Oh, you'd rather go to that little Bodn girl's than to come to me!"

"I didn't say that, and I didn't mean that, Kitty. I meant that I didn't want to do what you asked, because it wouldn't be polite or kind."

"Well, it seems to me, Laura Brooks, that you are putting on very ceremonious airs all at once. Didn't you postpone until another day a visit to Amy Stanton last winter, for just such a reason as this,--that you might go to Annie Grainger's when her mother went to Baltimore,--and Amy never thought of its being impolite or unkind."

"But that was different, Kitty."

"Different? Show me where the difference is, please."

"Oh, Kitty, you ***know***."

"But I ***don't*** know."

Laura's delicate face flushed a little, but after a moment's hesitation she said: "Esther is--is not like Amy Stanton or you; that is, she doesn't live in the same way.

The Bodns are poor,--quite poor, Kitty."

"Well, I don't see how that alters the case," still obstinately responded Kitty.

"Now, Kitty, you *do* see. Esther is shy and sensitive. She doesn't visit the people that we do."

"She doesn't visit *anybody*, so far as I know."

"Yes, that is just it," Laura went on eagerly; "and so you see that when she and her mother have made preparations for company--even one person--it would put them to a great deal of trouble and inconvenience to change the time, and it would be unkind and impolite to ask them to do it."

"How do you know that they have made such unusual preparations for you?" asked Kitty, sarcastically.

Laura flushed again as she answered: "I didn't mean unusual in one way, but I thought that they didn't often invite company by something that Esther said. When she asked me to fix a day, she told me that her mother wasn't very well, and that they didn't keep a servant."

"Not keep a servant! Not a single one! Why, they must be awfully poor, like common working-people!" exclaimed the young Beacon Street girl, in a wondering tone.

"Esther isn't common, if she is poor," Laura instantly asserted with decision.

"I don't understand how anybody so poor as that should be sent to Miss Milwood's school. I shouldn't think they could afford it," went on Kitty; "why, the place for her is a public school."

"But, Kitty, don't you know that Esther assists Miss Milwood,--that it is Esther who looks over all the French and German exercises, and makes the first corrections before mademoiselle takes them?"

"Esther Bodn?"

"Yes,--why, Esther, you must have noticed, is very proficient in French and German. She and her mother have lived abroad and here, in French and German families, to prepare her for being a teacher. She has a great natural aptitude, too, for languages."

"How in the world did you find all this out, Laura?"

"I didn't *find it out*, as you call it,--there is no secret about it,--Esther would no doubt have told you as much, if you had got as well acquainted with her as I have."

"I don't see how you came to get so well acquainted with her. She's nice enough, but I could always see that she wasn't like the rest of us,--of our set."

"Like the rest of us! She's just as good as the rest of us, and better than some of us."

"Oh, I dare say," said Kitty, in a patronizing tone.

"She may not be of our set, as you say, Kitty; but when I think of how Maud and Florence Aplin talk sometimes, I don't feel very proud of belonging to 'our set.'"

"Yes, I know, Maud and Flo do brag awfully now and then; but they are nice girls, and it is a nice family, mamma says."

"Every one seems to say that about them, and I've often wondered what they meant. I'm sure Mr. Aplin isn't very nice. He has no end of money, I know, but he can be so rude, and Mrs. Aplin is so patronizing. Now, why should they be called such 'nice people'?"

Kitty straightened herself up, put on a very knowing look, and repeated parrot-like what she had heard older persons say,--

"Mrs. Aplin was a Windlow."

"What in the world is a Windlow?" asked Laura, rather sarcastically.

Kitty was a worldly young woman, but she was also full of fun; and this question of Laura's amused her mightily, and with a suppressed giggle she answered demurely: "I think it has something to do with windows. The Windlows were English, and I believe their business was to open and shut the windows in the king's palaces,--perhaps to wash them. This all began ages ago, and it was considered a great honor, a tip-top thing to do, especially when the windows were high up. The honor has descended from generation to generation, and the name with it, I believe. They had some very ordinary name at the start."

The giggle, that had been suppressed up to this point, now burst forth in a shout of laughter, wherein Laura herself joined, exclaiming, as she did so, "Oh, Kitty, you are so ridiculous!"

"Why don't you make a rhyme and say, 'Oh, Kitty, you're so witty'? But, Laura, it is you who are odd and ridiculous, to pretend that you don't know that Windlow is one of the oldest names of one of the oldest families who came over to America in the Mayflower,--regular old aristocrats."

"Now, Kitty, I'm up in my history, if I'm not on this society stuff, and just let me tell you that those first settlers of America who came over in the Mayflower were *not* aristocrats."

"Oh, Laura, when everybody who can, brags of a Mayflower ancestor! I heard Mrs. Arkwright say to mamma, the other day that the Aplins were of the real old Mayflower blue blood."

"Then Mrs. Arkwright, with the 'everybody' you tell of, doesn't know what history says."

"Why, I'm sure I thought that was history."

"Well, it isn't. Last year I went with my father to Plymouth, and he took me to the famous rock where the Mayflower pilgrims landed, and afterward he gave me a lovely book called 'The Olden Time,' by Edmund Sears, that told me all about the pilgrims,--who they were, and why they came over, and everything, and I remember it said in this book that the Plymouth pilgrims were constantly confounded--those were the very words--with the Puritans who came over nine years later to Massachusetts."

"But Plymouth is in Massachusetts."

"Yes, I know, but it wasn't in that day. It was simply Plymouth Colony. The Mayflower sailed by Cape Cod into Plymouth Bay. They named the bay Plymouth, as they named the town Plymouth, for the old Plymouth in England."

"Did they name Cape Cod too?"

"No; that name was given years before by Captain Gosnold, an early voyager."

"Oh, I know, he caught such a lot of codfish there. I wish he'd never discovered the place; I hate codfish. But go on with your history lesson, Miss Brooks. I haven't any Mayflower ancestors, and so I'm more than resigned to have them taken down from their aristocratic peg."

"But they were lovely people,--lovely; kind and good to everybody, whether they believed as they did or not, for they had been persecuted themselves in the old country they had left for their opinions, and they meant that every one in the new country should worship as they pleased. They were very intelligent people, too, though, as this history says, 'from the middle and humbler walks of English life.' It was the men who came over to Massachusetts Bay and settled in Boston who were the aristocrats, and they were not nearly so liberal and generous as the Plymouth men. The head ones were stiff and overbearing, and meddled and interfered with people who didn't think as they did, and made a lot of strict little laws about all sorts of things, so that the name of 'Puritan' and 'puritanical' came to be used for anything that was bigoted and narrow-minded; and these names have stuck to all New England, and papa says that at this day people mix up things, and think that the Mayflower people and Boston people were all alike."

Kitty Grant gave a little hop, skip, and jump here, to Laura's astonishment. "Oh, Laura, it's such larks," she cried out. The two girls were walking down Beacon Street on their way home from school, and Laura looked about her to see what Kitty had so suddenly discovered to call out such an exclamation. Seeing nothing unusual, she asked, " ***What*** is such larks?"

Kitty laughed. "Oh, Laura, can't you see that this little fact you have pulled out from this tangled-up colony business, this dear dreadful little fact that the Mayflowers were not aristocrats, only--what does your history book say? Oh, I have it--'from the middle and humbler walks of English life;' not blue Mayflowers, but common colors--can't you see that it will be such larks for me to use this little fact like a little bombshell, when Mrs. Arkwright, or Maud, or Flo Aplin, or any of these Mayflower braggers begin to hold forth?"

"Why, Kitty, I thought you liked Maud and Flo!"

"I do when they don't give me too much Mayflower. I've always thought, and so has mamma, that this was their one fault,--that if it wasn't for that, they would be pretty near perfect; and now--and now, Brooksie, I shall proceed to be the means of grace that shall make them paragons of perfection. Oh, Laura, you're a treasure with that head of yours crammed full of facts, and I'll forgive you anything for this last little fact, even for neglecting me for that little Bodn girl!"

"I haven't neglected you."

"Well, snubbed me, then."

"Nor snubbed you. I only want to be considerate and polite to Esther; that's all."

"What a horrid name she has! Did you ever think of it, Laura--Esther Bodn--Bodn?"

"I don't think it's horrid at all. I like it."

"B-o-d-n--Bodn--it sounds awfully common."

"Why, Kitty, it's spelled B-o-w-d-o-i-n, the same as our Bowdoin Street, and pronounced Bod'n, as that is!"

"Is it, really? I didn't know that."

"I'm sure Bowdoin Street sounds well enough."

"Well, yes, I've always rather liked the sound of it; but then, you know, I always *saw* and *felt* the spelling, when I saw it. What in the world was the pronunciation ever snipped off like that for? It ought to be pronounced just as it is spelled. I've a good mind to pronounce it so the next time I speak to Esther."

"No, I wouldn't do that; but you might *think* of her as Miss Bowdoin," answered Laura, dryly.

"Oh, Laura, what a head full of wisdom you've got! I don't see how I ever lived without you. But--see here, tell me what street Miss Bowdoin lives in."

Laura hesitated a moment; then answered, "McVane Street."

"Where is McVane Street, for pity's sake? I never heard of it,--one of those horrid South End streets, I suppose?"

"No, it is at the West End, beyond Cambridge Street, down by the Massachusetts Hospital."

"No, no, Laura Brooks, you *don't* mean that she lives down there by the wharves?"

"It isn't by the wharves," cried Laura, indignantly.

"Well, it isn't far off. One of the regular old tumble-down streets, given up long ago to cobblers and tinkers of all kinds, and you're going to take tea with a girl who lives in that frowsy, dirty place!"

"It isn't frowsy and dirty. It's only an old, unfashionable street, but not frowsy or dirty. It's quite clean and quiet, and has shade-trees and little grass plots to some of the houses. Why, it used to be the court end of the town years ago."

"So was North Bennet Street, and all the rest of the North End; and now it's turned over to the rag-tag of creation,--Russian Jews, and every other kind of a foreigner,--and look here!" suddenly interrupting herself, as a new idea struck her, "I'll bet you anything that this Esther Bodn is a foreigner,--an emigrant herself of some sort."

"Kitty!"

"Yes, I'll bet you a pair of gloves,--eight-buttoned ones,--and I don't believe her name is spelled at all like our Bowdoin Street. I believe they--her mother and she--spell it that way ***to suit themselves***. I believe it's just Bodn; and that is an out-landish foreign name, if I--"

"Kitty, I think it's positively wicked for you to talk like this,--it's slander."

Kitty laughed, and, wagging her head to and fro, sang in a merry little under-tone,--

"Taffy is a Welshman, Taffy is a thief Flaunting as a Yankee man; that's my belief."

Laura couldn't help joining in this laugh, Kitty was so droll; but the laugh died out in the next breath, as she said,--

"Now, Kitty, don't go and talk like this to the other girls; don't--"

"Laura, how ***did*** it ever come about that the Bodn invited you to tea?" inter-rupted Kitty.

"It came about as naturally as this: One day I was going along Boylston Street, and just as I got to the public library I met Esther coming out with her arms full of books. I joined her, and insisted upon carrying some of the books for her; and after a little hesitation she accepted my offer, and led the way across the Common to the opposite gateway upon Charles Street. Here she stopped, and held out one hand for the books, and said, 'It was so kind of you to help me. Thank you very much.'

"'But I'm not going to leave you here,' I said; 'I'll walk home with you.' 'But it's a long walk to where I live,' she answered. I told her I didn't think anything of a long walk, and insisted on going further with her. I felt sorry, however, a minute after, for I saw that I had made a mistake,--that she didn't want me to go with her; but I didn't know how to turn back at once then, as she had started up briskly at my insistence with another 'Thank you.' But when we turned into Cambridge Street, I began to understand why she didn't want me,--she felt sensitive and afraid of my criticism; and I don't wonder--"

"Nor I, either," struck in Kitty, in a flippant tone.

"I should have felt sensitive," went on Laura, pityingly, "and I was so sorry for her; but I was determined to keep on then, and seem to take no notice, and some-how make her understand that it made no difference to me where she lived. I felt sorrier and sorrier for her, though, as she went on down Cambridge Street, past all those liquor and provision and second-hand furniture shops, with the tenements over them, and I was so thankful for her when she turned out of all this, and we crossed over and went into a quiet old street, and came out upon the pretty grounds of the Massachusetts Hospital; and as soon as I saw these grounds, I said, 'Oh, how pretty!' and then we turned again, and it was into the street opposite the hospital. It was almost as quiet as the country there. There were no shops at all, and the houses, though they looked old, were in very good repair, and some of them had been freshly painted, and had little grass plots beside them; and it was before one of these that Esther stopped, and then she said, 'If we had come over the hill, the way would have been pleasanter,' and I said just what I felt,--that I thought it was very pleasant, anyway, when you got there, and that the sunset must be beautiful from the windows. She was taking the books from me as I said this, and she looked up at me for a second, as if she were studying me, and then she asked me if I would like to come in some bright day, and see her and the sunsets,--that they were very beautiful from the upper windows. I told her I would like to come very much, and thanked her for asking me; and then I kissed her, for--"

"And struck up an intimate friendship at once," burst in Kitty, laughing.

"No, for this was some weeks ago, and she's only just asked me to set the day when I could come. Oh, Kitty, you may make fun all you like; but she is a very interesting girl,--my mother thinks she is too."

"Oh, you've introduced her to your mother, have you?"

"I have told mamma about her, and I brought her in one afternoon to see the pictures,--she's very fond of pictures,--and mamma asked her to stay to luncheon, but she couldn't."

"And now it is you who are going to make the first visit, going to sunsets and tea on McVane Street!"

"Laura! Laura!" called a voice here; and Laura looked up, to see her brother Jack in his T-cart pulling up at the curbstone. The next minute she was whirling off with him, bowing good-by to Kitty; and Kitty was calling after her mischievously,--

"Laura, Laura, tell your brother you are going to take tea with a girl who lives on McVane Street!"

CHAPTER II.

The spirited horse that young Jack Brooks drove held his attention so completely at that moment that he had no time to bestow upon anything else; but when he was well out on the broad, clear roadway of the "Neck," he turned to his sister, and asked, "What did Kitty Grant; mean by your going to take tea with a girl who lives on McVane Street?"

"It is one of the girls at Miss Milwood's school,--Esther Bodn."

"How does a girl who lives on McVane Street come to go to Miss Milwood's school?"

"She assists Miss Milwood." And Laura told what she knew of Esther's assistance in the way of the French and German.

"Oh!" and the young man gave a satisfied sort of nod as he uttered this, as much as to say, "That explains it;" and then, dismissing the subject from his mind, turned his whole attention again to his horse, while Laura drew a deep breath of relief. She had begun to think that if her brother were to take up Kitty's cry against McVane Street, she might find her anticipated visit set about with thorns. "But I shall go, I shall go!" she said to herself, "whatever Jack may say, when mamma says that I may."

But Jack said no more on that occasion, nor when his mother, the next day at luncheon, asked Laura what time Miss Bodn expected her, did the young gentleman make any remark. He had evidently forgotten the matter altogether; and Laura, without further anxiety, set out upon her little journey to McVane Street.

Kitty Grant had laughed that morning when Laura had told her that she was to go to Esther's at four o'clock and leave at six, that she might be in time for her own dinner hour,--had laughed and said, "Oh, a regular 'four-to-six,'--a sunset tea! The little Bodn is 'up' on 'sassiety' matters, isn't she? Dear me, I wish *I* could go with you,--I never went to a sunset tea. Couldn't you take me along?"

"No, I'm sure I couldn't," Laura had answered, laughing a little, but a little irritated, nevertheless, at Kitty's tone; and when Kitty had gone on and declared that nobody could be more appreciative than herself, Laura had retorted,--

"Yes; but you make great mistakes in your appreciations. You wouldn't appreciate Esther's own sweetness and refinement at their real worth, if the carpets and curtains and chairs and things in the house on McVane Street didn't happen to please your taste."

These words of hers returned to Laura with great force as the door of the house on McVane Street was opened to her, and she found herself in a chilly hall, darkly papered and darkly and shabbily carpeted; and when she followed Esther up the stairs,--for it was Esther who had answered her ring,--and noted the general dreariness of the whole, she thought pityingly, "Poor Esther, to be obliged to live in such a dismal fashion."

It was in this depressed state of mind that she came to the top of the stairs. Here Esther was waiting for her; and as she pushed wide open a door in front of her, she said brightly, "Here we are," and Laura, turning, stood for a moment dumb with surprise, as she saw a room that by contrast with the dinginess of the halls looked almost luxurious, for it was all lightness and brightness and warmth and sweet odors, with the sunshine streaming in upon a window full of plants, and touching up a quantity of woodcuts, photographs, and water-colors, with a few oils, and two or three fine etchings,--all of which pretty nearly hid the ugly dark wallpaper. A little coal fire in a low grate made things still brighter, and brought out the soft faded reds of the rug, and purples and yellows of the worn chintz covers of lounge and chairs. And right in the lightest and brightest spot of all this lightness and brightness stood a little claw-footed round table, bearing an old-fashioned tea-service of china. The sunshine seemed actually to fill up the cups and spill over into the gilt-bordered saucers, as Laura looked. "It is a 'sunset tea,' indeed," she said to herself; "and if Kitty Grant could see how pretty and refined were the simple arrangements, she wouldn't mix Esther up with any horrid common emigrants, if she *does* live on McVane Street. Esther a foreigner of any kind! Nothing could be more absurd. Esther was a New England girl, if ever there was one,--a little New England girl, who had come up with her mother to Boston from the Cape perhaps to learn to be a teacher. Yes, that must be the explanation of McVane Street. The Bodns were people who had come up from the country, and country people of small means wouldn't be likely to know where to choose a home."

Laura had all this settled satisfactorily in her mind after she had chatted awhile with Esther in the sunny room, and taken in more completely its various details, such as the fishnet drapery by the windows, the group of shells on the plant-stand, and several photographs of a sea-coast. And when shown other sea-country treasures,--bits of coral and ivory and mosses,--things grew plainer than ever, and she began to have a very clear notion of Esther's past surroundings, and pictured her mother as one of those neat, trim, anxious-faced little women she had often seen in her sea or mountain summerings. It was just when she had got this fancy picture sharply defined that she heard Esther say, as a door leading from the next room opened,--

"Mother dear, this is my friend Laura Brooks, I've told you about;" and Laura, rising hastily, turned to see no trim, anxious-faced little person, but a tall, handsome, dark-eyed woman smiling a greeting to her daughter's guest over the pot of tea and plate of bread and butter that she carried. Not in the least like the fancy picture; but who--who was it she suggested?

All through the little meal this question kept recurring to Laura. Where *had* she seen that dark, handsome face before? It recurred to her again, as she followed the mother and daughter up to the little third-story room, to see the beautiful sunset effects. Where *had* she seen just that profile against such a sunset light? Then all at once, as the declining beams sent a redder ray across the nose and chin, the question was answered. The red ray had also illumined Laura's own face, and Mrs. Bodn, turning suddenly, caught the girl's curiously animated expression, and asked inquiringly, "What is it, my dear?" and Laura answered eagerly,--

"Oh, do you know that picture of Walter Scott's 'Rebecca,' painted by some great English artist, I think? My uncle has a copy of it in his library, and it is so like you, *so* like you, Mrs. Bodn. The moment I saw you I was sure that I had met you before; but just now, when the sunset lit up your face, I knew at once what made it so familiar. It was its great resemblance to the 'Rebecca.' Oh, *do* you know the picture, Mrs. Bodn?"

"Yes, perfectly well," answered Mrs. Bodn, quietly; "but it was not painted by an English artist, it was the work of a young German who is now dead. He was very little known, though he did some fine work."

"And did you know that the picture was so like you, Mrs. Bodn?"

"Well, yes, I knew that it was thought to be like me when it was painted; and it ought to be, you know, for I sat for it,--I was the model."

"You were a--a--the model," gasped Laura, in astonishment.

"Yes, I was a--a--the model," answered Mrs. Bodn, repeating Laura's own halting syllables, with an accent half of amusement, half of sarcasm. Then, more seriously, she added, "It was years ago, when I was living in Munich."

"Esther, where are you?" a voice from the floor below here called out.

"We are up in your room looking at the sunset; it's lovely; come up and see it," Esther called back. And the next moment Laura was being introduced to "My cousin, David Wybern,"--a tall, good-looking boy of fifteen or sixteen, with beautiful dark eyes like Mrs. Bodn's. The next moment after that, when this tall, good-looking boy, in addressing Mrs. Bodn, called her "Aunt Rebecca," like a flash these thoughts went flying through Laura's mind,--

"A model for Rebecca the Jewess, and her own name Rebecca, and her daughter's and her nephew's names,--Esther, David,--these also Hebrew names!" What did it signify? Kitty--Kitty would say that it proved *she* was right,--that they *were* the very people she had said they were. But, oh, they were not; they were not of that common kind that Kitty had classed so scornfully! No matter if her mother *had* been a model years ago, it was through poverty, of course, and she was very brave not to be ashamed of it; and Esther,--Esther was lovely, a girl to be good to, to be true to, and she, Laura Brooks, would be good to her and true to her, no matter what happened. Poor Laura, she little knew how this resolve would be put to the test within the next few hours, for she could not foresee that the fact of the coachman's forgetfulness to call for her, as he had been ordered to do, and her consequent acceptance of David Wybern's attendance, was to bring such a storm about her. It had seemed the simplest thing in the world, when half-past six struck, and no carriage came for her, to accept David's attendance, and just as simple, when the street cars rushed by, without an inch of standing-room, to walk on and up over the hill to Beacon Street. But in this walk it happened that her brother had passed her as he drove by with one of his friends, and he had gone straight home and into the dining-room with the words, "What does this mean?" and then he proceeded to tell how he had passed his sister accompanied by a young man or boy who looked to him like one of the clerks in Weyman & Co.'s importing-house.

What did it mean, indeed? Her father and mother also wondered and exclaimed; and when Laura appeared, and told them what it meant, there was a general outcry of disapproval and criticism, led on by her brother, who told her she should have waited and sent a message to them by this boy, instead of permitting him to walk home with her. In vain Laura spoke of the boy's good manners, of the refined aspect of the little home which she had just visited, and the intelligence and dignity of Mrs. Bodn and her daughter. Nothing she said seemed to ameliorate the disapproval or criticism; and at last, stung by a sore sense of injustice, the girl turned upon her father and said, "Papa, I've always heard you say that everybody should be judged by their worth, and you've often and often quoted from that poem of Robert Burns that you are so fond of, about honest poverty, and I remember two lines particularly, that you seemed to like most of all,--

"'That sense and worth o'er a' the earth
    May bear the prize and a' that;'

"and yet now, now--"

"But, my dear child," as Laura here broke down with a little sob,--"my dear child, it isn't that these people are poor,--it is because we don't know anything about them."

"I--I think it is because you *do* know that--that they live on McVane Street," faltered Laura.

"Well, that *is* to know nothing about them, in the sense that father means," broke in her brother, sharply. "Their living there shows that they are the kind of people that are out of our class entirely,--people that we don't *want* to know. I didn't think it mattered much the other day, when you told me you were going down there to take tea with your teacher; but when I find you are to make friends with the young clerks who are the relations of your teacher, I think it matters a good deal."

"But this clerk, as you call him, has a great deal better manners than Charley Aplin. He behaves a great deal more like a gentleman."

"And he has a much longer nose," retorted her brother, with a sneering little laugh. "The fellow's a Jew, I'm certain; he has a regular Jewish face."

"He has *not*," began Laura, indignantly, and then stopped suddenly. It was the low trader-type of Jewish face reflected from her brother's mind that she saw as she spoke; then Mrs. Bodn's beautiful profile and that of her nephew rose before her! If they--if they--her brother, her father, could see these faces,--these faces so fine and intelligent, and saw, too, the likeness that she had seen to the portrait in her uncle's library,--would they feel differently,--would they do justice to Esther and her relations, though they *were* Jews,--would they admit that they were of the higher type, that they were fit friends for her? No, no, no, she answered herself, as soon as these questions started up in her mind, and, stung through all her generous young heart by these instinctive answers, she burst forth: "You talk about Jews as if there were but one class,--the lowest class. What if all Americans were judged by the lowest class? Would you call that fair? And you think the Bodns are the lowest kind just because they are poor and live on McVane Street! That great novelist who lived in England and who was prime minister there, Lord Beaconsfield, was a Jew, and he was proud of it; and the Mendelssohns were Jews; and there are those wonderful musical novels Uncle George gave me to read last summer, 'Charles Auchester' and 'Counterparts,' they are full of Jews and their genius--"

"Laura, Laura, there is no need of your talking like this," interrupted her father; "we are not going to deny the worth or respectability of your new acquaintances, but it is entirely unnecessary for you to rush into any intimacy with such strangers."

There was a look in her father's face, as he spoke, that told Laura very plainly that all she had said had done more harm than good, and that henceforth there would be no more "sunset teas" with Esther Bodn. All her little plans, too, for making Esther's life brighter, by welcoming her into her own home, and bringing her into a better acquaintance with the other girls, were rendered impossible now. But if she could not be good to her in this way, she would be more than ever kind and cordial to her at school, and she would try to enlist Kitty Grant's interest. She would tell Kitty about that pretty refined home, and ask her to be kind and cordial too; and she was sure that Kitty would not refuse, for, in spite of her fun and her worldliness, Kitty had really a kind heart. Yes, she would enlist Kitty, and Kitty was all powerful. If she once got interested in a person, she could make everybody else interested. But, alas, for this scheme!

CHAPTER III.

Alas! because Kitty had already taken her stand on the other side. She had already told the girls that Esther Bodn lived on McVane Street, in near neighborhood to a lot of rum-shops and foreigners, and had then "made fun," in the same rattling way that she had used with Laura, airing all her little suspicions and suggestions about the name of Bodn, in the half-frolic fashion that always had such effect upon the listeners. It had such effect on this occasion, that Laura found that every girl had passed from indifference to an active prejudice against Esther. Kitty herself had not meant to produce this result. Indeed, Kitty had had no meaning whatever but that of amusing herself,--"making fun;" and when the girls, relishing this "fun," laughed and applauded, she did not realize that she had done a mischievous thing. Poor Laura, however, realized everything as the days went by, and she saw Esther subjected to a certain critical observation. Her only hope was that the person most interested did not notice this; but one day she came upon Esther at recess, bending over a pile of exercises, at which she was apparently hard at work.

"What's the rush, Esther, that you've got to work at recess?" she asked.

Esther murmured an unintelligible reply, and bent her head still lower; and then it was that Laura, to her dismay, saw a tear drop to the exercises upon the desk.

"Esther, Esther, what is the matter? Tell me!"

"I--I don't know," faltered Esther, "but things seem different. I always knew that the girls didn't care very much for me, but they were not unkind. Now--they--seem unkind some way. Perhaps it's only my fancy, but--but they seem to look down on me as they didn't before, and--and sometimes they seem to avoid me, and--I'm just the same as ever, except--except I'm a good deal shabbier this spring. I've always been rather shabby, but this spring it's worse, because we've lost some money,--not much, but it was a good deal to us, and I couldn't have anything new; and--and there's another thing--one morning I overheard one of the girls say to Kitty Grant, 'McVane Street, that is enough!' They must have been talking about me and where I live. Nobody else here lives on McVane Street, and we--mother and

I--wouldn't live there if we could afford to live where we liked; but we came here strangers, and this was much the most comfortable place we could find for what we could pay. I know it's in a disagreeable part of the city; but it ***isn't*** bad, it ***isn't*** low, where we are, it's only run down and shabby. But I thought Boston people were above judging others by such things. I'd always heard that Boston girls--"

"Boston girls! oh, don't talk to me of Boston girls, don't talk to me of any girls anywhere," burst in Laura. "I'm sick--sick of girls. Girls will do things and say things--little, mean, petty things--that boys would be ashamed to do or say."

"Then you ***do*** think it's because of my shabbiness and where I live that--that has made them--these girls so--so different; but why should they--all at once? I can't understand."

"Don't try to understand! Don't bother your head about them--they don't mean--they don't know--they are not worth your notice. You are a long, long way above them!"

"Mother didn't want to come to Boston to live; but when my uncle John Wybern, mother's brother, died three years ago,--he died in Munich; he was an artist, like my father, and we'd all lived together, since my father's death,--we came on here, as uncle had advised, because he knew some one here in an importing-house who would get David a situation. He didn't want David to be an artist. He said it was such an anxious, hand-to-mouth life, if one didn't make a quick success of it; and ***he knew***, for ***he*** hadn't made a success any more than my father had,--and--and this is why we came here, and are here now on McVane Street, though my mother didn't want to come. But ***I*** wanted to come from the first. I'd heard and read so much about Boston, I thought I was sure to be happy here, for I thought the people were so noble and high-minded, and--" There was a pathetic little faltering break again at this, which was resolutely repressed, and the sentence resumed with, "and then I knew my father's people had once--" But at this point, "Esther," called out Miss Milwood from the doorway, "bring the exercises into my room, and we'll finish them together."

Almost at that very moment Kitty Grant came running down the aisle, calling out, "Laura, Laura, are you going this afternoon to the Art Club?"

"To hear Monsieur Baudouin? Yes."

"Well, we'll go together, then."

"Very well."

"Very well," mimicking Laura's cool tones; then with a change of voice, "Laura, what *is* the matter? You are enough to freeze anybody. What have I done?"

"You've done a very cruel thing."

"Laura!"

"Yes, I sha'n't take back my words,--you have done a very cruel thing."

"For pity's sake, what do you mean?"

"You may well say 'for *pity's* sake;'" and then Laura burst forth and repeated, word for word, the conversation that had transpired between Esther and herself, concluding with, "And you--*you*, Kitty, are to blame for this, for it is you who have prejudiced the girls against Esther with your talk about McVane Street and the foreigners in that neighborhood."

"I? Just my little fun about McVane Street and your sunset tea there?"

"Yes, just your little fun! I know what your fun is! Oh, Kitty, Kitty, I *did* think you had a kind heart! But to be the means of hurting anybody, as you have hurt Esther,--it is--it is--"

"Laura, Laura, don't," as Laura here broke down in a little fit of sobbing. "Of course I didn't know--I didn't think. Oh, dear, I'll tell the girls I didn't mean a word I said,--that I'm the biggest liar in town; that Esther is an heiress; that--that--oh, I'll do or say anything, if you'll only stop crying, Laura. There, there," as Laura tried to stifle a fresh sob, "that's right, take my handkerchief,--yours is sopping wet, and-- My goodness, there comes Maud Aplin--she *must* not see us sniffing and sobbing like this, she'll say we've had a quarrel. Here, let us go into the little recitation-room, quick now, before she sees us."

And into the little recitation-room Laura was very willing to go and hide her tear-stained face from inquisitive eyes, while Kitty, penitent and overcome more by the spectacle of these tears than by a sense of her own shortcomings, followed briskly after, with this cheerful little running fire of remarks, anent the Art Club lecturer: "I'm just crazy--*crazy* to see this Monsieur Baudouin; for what do you think Flo Aplin says? That he is a real viscomte or marquis, or something of that sort, but that he came into his title only a year or two ago, and is much prouder of his reputation as an art authority and critic and his name, Pierre Baudouin,--it's his own name, you know,--and he won his reputation under that. The Aplins met him last year in Paris. Windlow Aplin, who is studying art there, just swears by him, and says the artists dote on him, and Flo says he is perfectly elegant. Etching is his great fad now, and he is going to lecture this afternoon on etching and etchers. Oh, I'm just crazy to see and hear him, aren't you?"

Laura had by this time conquered her tears, thanks to Kitty's adroitness, and, with a half-humorous, half-grateful appreciation of this adroitness, she thought to herself as she walked round to the Art Club with Kitty that afternoon, "Kitty *has* a good heart, after all."

The Art Club hall was quite full as they entered; but there were seats well down in front, and there they found most of the school girls under Miss Milwood's charge. Esther was one of this party; and Kitty made a great point of leaning forward and bowing to her with much graciousness. The next moment she was whispering to Laura, "There, didn't I behave prettily to Esther this time? You'll see now--" But at that instant a slender dark-eyed gentleman, accompanied by one of the artists, was seen coming rapidly up the aisle, and, "Look, look, there he is!" cried Kitty, "and *isn't* he elegant?"

And Laura looking, as she was told, found no reason to disagree with this comment.

"But I *do* hope," whispered the irrepressible Kitty again, as Monsieur Baudouin ascended the platform,--"I *do* hope he is as interesting as he looks; appearances are deceitful sometimes." But no one of that audience found Pierre Baudouin's appearance deceitful. He was more than interesting,--he was enthralling as he went on with his almost loving consideration of his subject, setting before his hearers, in a melodious voice and very good English, some of the results of his great knowledge and experience. You could have heard a pin drop, as the saying goes, so spell-bound was the audience; and at the end there was a warm outburst of applause, and then a gathering about him, as he left the platform, of the various artists, and others who were eager to speak with him. He was standing with this little group, when Laura, watching and listening just outside of it, heard him say, "There is a remarkable etching that I wish I could show you, for it proves completely the theory I have just placed before you. I saw it but once, in the artist's own studio, as I was passing through Munich. When a little later I heard that the artist was dead, and his effects for sale, I tried to buy the etching, but was told that it had been given to a friend, a

Mr. John Wybern. Since then, I have learned that Mr. Wybern has also died, and I started again on my search; but it has been fruitless so far, though I still hope I may come across it, and be able, if not to add it to my collection, to examine it again. The artist, by the way, is the same one that painted that remarkable picture, 'Rebecca the Jewess.'"

Laura turned hastily around to look for Esther. She had not to look far. Esther was just behind her. "Esther, did you hear?" she asked.

Esther nodded.

"Do you know about the etching?"

"Yes, it hangs in our parlor. I wish I dared go forward now and tell him."

"Oh, Esther, do, do!"

But Esther hung back. Then Laura obeyed an impulse that forever after filled her with astonishment. She pressed forward, and, before she had time to think twice, was addressing Monsieur Baudouin, and telling him what she knew.

"What! you can tell me where this etching is? You can take me to it?" he exclaimed, with a sort of joyful incredulity.

Laura answered by turning to Esther and saying. "This young lady can tell you more about it. The etching is in the possession of her family."

"Ah, and this young lady is--"

Laura reached back, seized Esther's hand, and pulled her to her side.

"Is Miss Bodn."

"Mees **Bodn**!" he repeated with a start. "Mees **Bodn**! Ah, pardon me, do you spell this name B-o-w-d-o-i-n?"

"You do, you do," as Esther answered in the affirmative; "and, pardon again, are you related to one Henri--Henry, you call it here--Henry Pierre Bowdoin?"

"My father's name was Henry Pierre Bowdoin."

"Then, Mademoiselle," and Monsieur Baudouin stretched out his hand, and a smile lit up his face, "you must be a relation of mine; and three years ago, when I was in this country, and tried to find the American branch of our family that spelled its name Bowdoin and was called Bodn, but which was originally Baudouin, the old Huguenot name, I was told it had died out. Where were you then, Mademoiselle?"

"In Munich, where my mother and I had lived with my uncle John Wybern, since my father's death, years ago."

"Your uncle! John Wybern was your uncle? So--so is it possible, is it possible? And I find the two objects I have been hunting, so far apart, together! It is most astonishing and yet most simple. And your mother--your mother is living? Yes, and you will give me your address, that I may hasten to pay my respects to her;" and Monsieur whipped out a little note-book and wrote down, probably with greater satisfaction than it had ever been written before, "McVane Street."

"Most astonishing and yet most simple," as Monsieur had truly said; yet to the flock of Miss Milwood's girls, who, well down to the front, had lost nothing of this surprising interview, it was only "most astonishing," and to some of them most humiliating and mortifying. Kitty Grant was the first to voice this mortification, by turning upon them and saying, as Esther disappeared with Monsieur Baudouin, "Say, girls, how do you feel now? *I* feel like one of Cinderella's sisters. Laura now-- Laura, where are you?" But Laura had also disappeared. She wanted to be by herself and think it over. But what of Esther,--Esther, who had been neglected and disregarded and despised? What of Esther, as she stood there, and as she walked away with Monsieur Baudouin? Esther was the least astonished of them all, for years ago she had been familiar with the facts of her paternal family history, and knew that she was a descendant of Pierre Baudouin, a French Huguenot, who had fled to America to escape religious persecution, and knew that the name Baudouin had suffered a change to Bowdoin; knew, too, that as Bowdoin it had been made illustrious in America's annals, and worn the honors of the highest offices of the State. She knew all this; but she knew also that this was long ago, and that her father was the last of his name in America, and when he died, after a wasting illness that exhausted his fortune, there was little thought given to the fact that the old Huguenot root still existed in France, though half-playful, half-serious mention had now and then been made of the kinsfolk in France they would sometime go to seek.

All this Esther had stored away in her memory, so that when Monsieur Baudouin announced himself as the kinsman from France, it was more like a long-anticipated event than a surprise. And all this she told to Laura in the days that followed,--those dear, delightful days, when there was no difficulty put in the way of going to McVane Street; when McVane Street, indeed, according to Kitty, became quite the fashion with the artists flocking to see the wonderful etching, and Monsieur Baudouin holding forth upon its merits to them as he made himself at home with his American kinsfolk, who were now discovered to be such charming folk. Laura sometimes in these days blazed up with indignation and disgust as she noted the sudden attentions that were bestowed upon Esther and her mother. No one now spoke of emigrants and foreigners in connection with these dwellers on McVane Street. Jack Brooks himself seemed to forget that David Wybern looked like a Jew, even before it was found that David and all of his people were of the most unmixed Puritan stock!

"And I, too," thought Laura,--"I, too, muddled and mistook things as I shouldn't, if Esther and her mother had lived in a different quarter. If they had lived anywhere over the hill, should I have fancied, though they *were* so poor, that Mrs. Bowdoin must have been a professional model? No, no, I should have thought at once, what I *know* now, that the artist was her friend, and that she sat to him as a friendly favor, like any other lady."

But while Laura thus scourged herself with the rest, Esther and her mother had set her apart from all the rest for their special love and confidence,--a love and confidence that are as fresh to-day as when the mother and daughter sailed away with Monsieur Baudouin, a year ago, to visit their French kinsfolk.

BECKY.
CHAPTER I.

"Number five!" called out shrilly and impatiently the saleswoman at the lace counter in a great dry-goods establishment. The call was repeated in a still more impatient tone before there was any response; then there rushed up a girl of ten or eleven, whose big black eyes looked forth fearlessly, some people said impudently, from a little peaked face, so thin and small that it seemed all eyes, and in the neighborhood where the child lived she was often nicknamed "Eyes."

"Why didn't you come when you were first called?" asked the saleswoman, angrily.

"Couldn't; I'se waitin' for somethin'," answered the child, coolly.

"You were staring at and list'nin' to those ladies at the ribbon counter; I saw you," retorted the saleswoman.

"Well, I tole yer, I'se waitin' for somethin'," the girl answered, showing two rows of teeth in a mischievous grin.

A younger saleswoman, standing near, giggled.

"Don't laugh at her, Lizzie," rebuked the elder; "she's getting too big for her boots with her impudence."

"They ain't boots; they're shoes." And a thin little leg was thrust forward to show a foot encased in a shabby old shoe much too large for it.

Then, like a flash, the "imp," as the saleswoman often termed her, seized the parcel that was ready for her, and darted off with it.

"You'll get reported if you don't look out," the saleswoman called after her.

The "imp" turned her head and winked back at the irritated saleswoman in such a grotesque fashion that the lively Lizzie giggled again, for which she was told she ought to be ashamed of herself. Good-natured Lizzie admitted the truth of this accusation, but declared that Becky was so funny she "just couldn't help laughing."

"You call it 'funny,'" the other exclaimed; "*I* call it impudence. She ain't afraid of anything or anybody. Look at her now! there she is back at the ribbon counter. I wonder what those swells are talking about, that she's so taken up with. She's up to some mischief, I'll bet you, Lizzie."

"I guess it's only her fun. She's going to take 'em off by 'n' by," said Lizzie.

This was one of the "imp's" accomplishments,--taking people off. She was a great mimic, and on rainy days when the girls ate their luncheon in the room that the firm had allotted to them for that purpose, Miss Becky would "take off," the various people that had come under her keen observation during the day. "Private theatricals," the lively Lizzie called this "taking off," as Becky strutted and minced, with her chin up, her dress lifted in one hand, while with the other she held a pair of scissors for an eyeglass, and peered through the bows at a piece of cloth, which she picked and pecked and commented upon in fine-lady fashion,--"just like the swells," Lizzie declared. It was quite natural then for her to conclude that it was fun of this sort that Becky was "up to," in her close attention to the "swell" customers at the ribbon counter. "She was studyin' 'em, just as actresses study their play-parts," Lizzie thought to herself; and half an hour later, when she met Becky in the lunch-room, she called out to her,--

"Come, Becky, give us the swells at the ribbon counter."

"Eh?" said Becky.

Lizzie repeated her request, and the other girls joined in: "Yes, Becky, give us the swells at the ribbon counter; we want some fun."

"They warn't funny," answered Becky, shortly.

"Oh! now, Becky, what'd you stand there lis'nin' and lookin' at 'em so long for?"

"'Cause they were sayin' somethin' I wanted to hear."

"Of course they were. What was it about, Becky?"

"May-day, flowers and queens and baskets."

"Oh, my! Well, tell us how they said it, Becky."

"I tole yer they warn't funny; they warn't o' that kind that peeks through them long stick glasses and puckers up their lips. They talked straight 'long, and said very int'restin' things," said Becky.

"Well, tell us; tell us what 'twas," exclaimed Lizzie.

"Oh, you wouldn't care for what they's talkin' 'bout. They warn't sayin' anythin' 'bout beaux or clothes," Becky replied with a grin.

A shout of laughter went up from the rest of the company, who all knew the lively Lizzie's favorite topics. Lizzie joined in the laugh, and cried good-naturedly,--

"Never mind, Becky, if I'm not up to your ribbon swells talk; tell us about it."

"Oh, yes! tell us, tell us!" echoed the others.

Becky took a bite out of a slice of bread, and munching it slowly, said,--

"I tole yer once 't was 'bout May-day and flowers and queens and baskets."

"What May-day? There's thirty-one of 'em, Becky."

Becky looked staggered for a moment. In her little hard-worked life she had had small opportunity to learn much out of books, and she had never happened to hear this rhyming bit:--

"Thirty days hath September, April, June, and November, All the rest have thirty-one,   Excepting February alone."

Recovering her wits, however, very speedily, she said coolly,--

"The first pleasant one."

"Well, what were they telling about it? What were they going to do the first pleasant day in May?"

"They didn't say as *they* was goin' to do anythin'; they was tellin'--or one of 'em was tellin' t' other one--what folks did when they's little, and afore that, hundreds o' years ago, how the folks then used to get all the children together and go out in the country and put up a great big high pole, and put a lot o' flowers on a string and wind 'em roun' the pole; and then all the children would take hold o' han's and dance roun' the pole, and one o' the children was chose to be queen, and had a crown made o' flowers on her head, and the rest o' the children minded her."

"You'd like *that*,--to be queen and have the rest mind you, Becky, wouldn't you?" laughed one of the company.

"I bet I would," owned Becky, frankly.

"But what about the baskets?" asked somebody else.

"Oh, the kids," said Becky, forgetting in her present absorbed interest the term "children,"--which she had learned to use since she had come up daily from the poor neighborhood where she lived,--"the kids use to fill a basket with flowers and hang it on the door-knob of somebody's house,--somebody they knew,--and then ring the bell and run. Golly! guess *I* should hev to hang it *inside* where I lives. I couldn't hang it on no outside door and hev it stay there long,--them thieves o' alley boys would git it 'fore yer could turn. I guess, though, they was country kids who used to hang 'em; but the lady said she was goin' to try to start 'em up again here in the city."

"What kind o' baskets were they?" asked Lizzie, suddenly sitting up with a new air of attention.

"Oh, ho!" laughed one of the girls; "Lizzie wants to hang a basket for some-body *she* knows!"

"Hush up!" said Lizzie, turning rather red. Then, addressing Becky again: "Did the lady who was telling about 'em have a basket with her? Did you see it?"

"No, but she hed a piece o' that pretty wrinkly paper jes' like the lamp-shades in the winders, and she said the baskets was made o' that, and she was buyin' some ribbon to match for handles and bows."

"Oh, I *wish* I could see one of 'em," said Lizzie.

"I went to a kinnergarden school wonst when I was a little kid," struck in Becky here, "and we was put up there to makin' baskets out o' paper."

"Could you do it now?" asked Lizzie, eagerly.

"Mebbe I could," answered Becky, warily; "but it's a good bit ago."

"When you were young," cried one of the company with a giggle.

"Yes, when I was young," repeated Becky, in exact imitation of the speaker, whose voice was very flat and nasal.

Everybody laughed, and one of the girls cried: "Becky'll get the best of you any time." They were all of them impressed with this fact, when, a few minutes after, the wary Becky agreed to show Lizzie what she knew of "kinnergarden" basket-making, if Lizzie would agree to pay her for her trouble by giving her materials enough to make a basket for herself.

"Ain't she a sharp one?" commented one of the girls to another when they had left the lunch-room.

"Ain't she, though? She'll get what she can, and hold on to what she's got every time."

"But she's awful good fun. Didn't she take off Matty Kelley's flat nose-y way of talkin' to a T?"

"Didn't she!" and the two girls laughed anew at the recollection.

CHAPTER II.

Becky was the only one of the parcel-girls who was in the lunch-room when this talk about May-day took place. The others lived nearer to the store, and had gone home to their dinners. They were all a trifle older than Becky, and a good deal larger. For these reasons, as well as for the fact that they had been in the establishment quite a while when Becky entered it, they had put on a great many disagreeable airs toward the pale-faced little girl when she first appeared, and attempted, as Becky put it, to "boss" her. They soon found, however, that the new-comer was too much for them. They expected her to be afraid of them,--to "stand round" for them. But Miss Becky was not in the least afraid of them, or, for that matter, of anybody; and as soon as she understood what they meant, she turned upon them the whole force of that inimitable mimicry of hers, and "took off" their airs in a manner that soon set the small army of salesmen and saleswomen into such fits of laughter that the tables were completely turned upon the tormentors, and they were only too glad to drop their airs and treat Becky with the respect that pluck and superior power invariably command. But while thus constrained to decent behavior before Becky's eyes, behind her back they gave way to the resentment that they felt against her for her triumph over them, and let no opportunity slip to say slighting things of her. Good-natured Lizzie would laugh when they said these things to her,--when they told her that Becky Hawkins was nothin' but one o' that low lot who lived down amongst that thieving set by the East Cove alleys,--that jus' as like as not she was a thief herself; that she was awful close and stingy, anyway, and saved up every scrap she could find; that they'd seen her themselves pick up old strings and buttons and such duds from the gutters! But if Lizzie laughed out of her light lively heart, and declared she didn't believe what they said was true, and didn't care if it *was*, there were others not so good-natured as Lizzie, who, though often vastly entertained by Becky, were quite ready to believe that the spirit of mimicry she possessed had something lawless about it, especially when she broke forth into the slang of the street,--"gutter-slang," the other parcel-girls called it,--the lawlessness seemed to gather a sort of proof. And so it was that, in spite of the entertainment she afforded, and a certain kind of respect in which her "smartness" was held, Becky was considered as rather an outsider, and an object of more or less suspicion.

"A sharp one!" the saleswoman had called her, the other agreeing; and when the next day, which was also a rainy day, the little company gathered in the lunch-room again, and Lizzie brought forth a variety of pretty papers, there was a general watchfulness to see how much Becky knew, and what she would claim. Two other of the parcel-girls were now present. They had heard all about the basket-making plan of yesterday, and pushed forward with great interest. Becky looked at them with mischief in her eyes, but made no movement to join Lizzie.

"Come," said the older of the two, "why don't you begin, Becky? Lizzie's waitin', and so are we."

"What *yer* waitin' for?" asked Becky, with an impudent grin.

"To see how you make the baskets."

"Well, yer'll hev to wait."

"Why, you told Lizzie you'd show her how to make baskets out o' paper!"

"But I didn' say I'se goin' to show anybody else. This ain't a free kinnergarden. These are private lessons."

A shriek of laughter went up at this, while somebody cried,--

"And private lessons must be paid for, mustn't they, Becky?"

"Every time," answered Becky, with unruffled coolness.

"Where's the private room to give 'em in?" piped out one of the parcel-girls with a wink at the other.

"In here!" cried Becky, with a sudden inspiration, jumping up and running into a little fitting-room that had that morning been assigned to her to sweep and put in order after the lunch hour.

"Good for you!" cried Lizzie, with one of her laughs, as she followed her teacher.

"And you didn't get ahead o' me *this* time, either!" called out Becky, as she bolted the door upon herself and companion.

"You're too sharp for any of *us*, Becky," called back one of the saleswomen.

"*Ain't* she sharp?" agreed one and another; and "I told you so," said still another. "She's a regular little cove-sharper, as Lotty said." Lotty was the older parcel-girl.

And thus, though most of them laughed at Becky's last "move," they were prejudiced against her for it, and thought it another evidence of her stinginess and sharpness. They all agreed, however, that she had "got 'round' Lizzie to that extent that that young woman would stand up for her, anyway, no matter what she'd do or didn't do.

"An' I'll bet yer," said the younger parcel-girl, "she'll lie out o' that basket biz-ness, an' get a lot o' paper too. *She* know how to make baskets! Not much. You see now when they come out o' the fitting-room there'll be some excuse that 't ain't done, an' they can't show it now,--you see."

This prophecy was received in silence, but without much sign of disagreement; and when the fitting-room door finally opened, it was funny to watch the looks of astonishment that were bestowed upon the pretty little basket of green and white paper that Lizzie held swung upon her finger.

"Well, I never! She *did* know how, didn't she?" exclaimed one of the party.

"Of course she did," answered Lizzie.

Becky only shrugged her shoulders disdainfully.

"Bet yer she hooked it out o' some shop, and had it in that bag she carried in," whispered Lotty Riker, the parcel-girl.

"Hush!" warned one of the company.

But it was too late. Becky had heard, and for the first time since she had been in the store, those about her saw hot wrath blazing from her eyes as she burst forth savagely,--

"Yer mean low-lived thing yer, yer must be up to sech tricks yerself to think that!"

"What is it? What did she say?" asked Lizzie.

Becky repeated Lotty's words, her wrath increasing as she did so.

"Hooked it! You know better, and you ought to be ashamed of yourself, Lotty Riker," said Lizzie. "Becky and I made the basket ourselves. See here now!" and, opening one hand, she displayed the ends of the paper strips as they had been cut off, and where they fitted the protruding ends on the basket. "But," turning to Becky, "Lotty knows better; she only wanted to bother you."

"She wanted to bully me! She's been at it ever since I come here,--she and t' other one. I made 'em stop it wonst, an' I'll make 'em ag'in. I can stan' a good deal, but I ain't a-goin' to stan' bein' called a thief, I ain't. I ain't no more a thief 'n they be, if I do live down Cove way, and don't wear quite so good clo'es as they does. *Hooked it*!" going a step nearer to the two girls. "I wish we was boys. I'd--I'd lick yer, I would, the minit I got yer out on the street; but," with a disgusted sigh, "I'm a girl, and I carn't. 'Tain't 'spectable for girls, Tim says, an' I mus'n't. But lemme jes' hear any more sech talk, an'--I'll *forgit I'm a girl for 'bout five minutes*!"

This conclusion was too much for Lizzie's gravity, and she burst into one of her infectious laughs. Several of the others joined in, and then Becky herself gave a sudden little grin.

Lotty Riker and her sister, who had been thoroughly frightened, felt immensely relieved at this, and for the moment everything seemed the same as before the outbreak; but it was only seeming. The majority of the company, without taking into consideration the provocation Becky had received, thought to themselves: "*What* a temper!" Becky's wild little threats, and the way she expressed herself, had made a strong impression; and when presently Lizzie laughingly asked, "Who's Tim, Becky?" and Becky had answered in that lawless manner of hers: "Oh, he's a fren' o' mine,--a great big fightin' gentleman what lives in the house where we do," there was a general exchange of glances, and a general conviction that the Riker girls had not been altogether wrong in some of their statements. And when the next day they heard Miss Becky confide to Lizzie that she had made "a splendid basket," and was going to hang it for Tim on that "fust pleasant day of May," they whispered to each other, "A May-basket for a prize-fighter!"

But they took very good care that the whisper did not reach Becky. She was "great fun," but they had found out how fiercely she could turn from her fun.

CHAPTER III.

The first day of May turned out to be a most beautiful day, bright and sunny; and when Lizzie hung her pretty basket filled with Plymouth Mayflowers on the door-knob of a great friend of hers, she laughed, and wondered if Becky had hung hers for that "fightin' gen'leman, Tim." She would ask Becky the minute she got to the store. But the minute she got to the store she had a customer to wait upon, and had no time to bestow on Becky until she needed her service. Then she called "Number Five;" but, instead of "Number Five," Lotty Riker responded.

"Where's Becky?" asked Lizzie.

"I dunno. She hain't come in; mebbe she's hangin' that May-basket for the prize-fighter," giggled Lotty.

Business was very brisk that day, and Lizzie had no leisure for anything else. But at noon, when she was going out to her lunch, it occurred to her that Becky had not yet appeared. Where *could* she be? She had always been punctual to a minute.

The afternoon was busier than the morning, and once more Becky was forgotten. It was not until the closing hour--five o'clock--that Lizzie thought of her again, and then she burst out to Matty and Josie Kelly, as they were leaving the store together,--

"Where *do* you suppose Becky Hawkins is? She hasn't been here to-day, and she's *always* here, and so punctual."

"Mebbe she's taken it into her head to leave," answered Matty. "'T would be just like her; she's that independent."

"Catch her leaving when she'd have anything to lose. She'd lose a week's pay to leave without warning, and she knows it. She's too sharp to do that," put in Josie, laughing,

"I hope she ain't sick," said Lizzie.

"Sick! *her* kind don't get sick easy. Those Cove streeters are tough. Lizzie, how much did she get out of you for showing you how to make that basket?"

"Why, what I agreed to give,--enough to make a basket for herself; and last night, when she was going home, I gave her some of my Mayflowers,--I had plenty."

"Well, I'm sure you are real generous."

"No, I'm not; it was a bargain."

"Yes, *Becky's* bargain, and she'd like to have made a bargain with the rest of us. The idea of taking you off into that fitting-room, so't the rest of us wouldn't profit by her showing you, and then her talking about private lessons!"

"Oh, that was only her fun."

"Fun! and when one of the girls said, 'And private lessons must be paid for, mustn't they, Becky?' and she answered, 'Yes, every time,' do you think that was only fun?"

"Yes; and if it wasn't, I don't care. She's a right to make a little something if she can. They're awful poor folks down there on Cove Street."

"Make a little something! Yes, but I guess you wouldn't catch any of the other girls here making a little something like that out of the friends she was working alongside of."

"Friends!" exclaimed Lizzie.

"And say, Lizzie," went on Josie, paying no attention to Lizzie's exclamation, "I'll bet you anything she *sold* her basket, and very likely to that prize-fighter,--that Tim."

"I don't care if she did. But don't let's talk any more about her. I hate to talk about folks, and it doesn't do any good to think bad things of 'em. But, hark, what's that the newsboys are crying? 'Awful disaster down--' Where? Stop a minute, I'm going to buy a paper."

"Yes, here it is, awful disaster down in one of the Cove Street tenement-houses," read Lizzie; and then, bringing up suddenly, she cried, "Why, girls, girls, that's where Becky lives,--in one of those tenements."

"Go on, go on!" urged Matty; and Lizzie went on, and read: "'At six o'clock this morning one of the most disastrous fires that we have had for years broke out in the rear of the Cove Street tenement-houses, and, owing to the high wind and the dryness of the season, it had gained such headway by the time the engines arrived, that it looked as if not only the whole block but the adjoining buildings were doomed; but after hours of untiring effort on the part of the firemen, it was finally brought under control. Several of the tenements were completely gutted, and the wildest excitement prevailed as the panic-stricken tenants, with cries and shrieks of terror, jumped from the windows, or in other ways sought to save themselves. It is not yet ascertained how many lost their lives in these attempts, but it is feared that the number is by no means small.'"

"I'm going down there! I'm going down there!" Lizzie cried out here, breaking off her reading, and starting forward at a rapid pace.

"But, Lizzie--"

"You needn't try to stop me, I'm *going*. Becky's down there somewhere, and mebbe she's alive and hurt and needs something, and I'm going to see. *You* needn't come if you're afraid, but *I'm* going!"

The two girls offered no further remonstrance, but silently turned; and the three went on together toward the burned district.

"What yer doin' here?" asked a policeman gruffly, as they entered Cove Street. "Go back! 't ain't no place for anybody that hain't got business here."

"I'm looking for little Becky Hawkins,--one of the girls in our store," answered Lizzie.

"Becky Hawkins?"

"Yes; do you know her?"

"Should think I did. This is my beat,--known her all her life pretty much."

"Did she get out,--is she alive?" asked Lizzie, breathlessly.

"Yes, she's alive; she's down there in that corner house with her friend Tim."

The policeman's lips moved with a faint odd smile as he said this,--a smile that Matty and Josie interpreted to mean that Becky was just what the Riker girls had said she was,--a little Cove Street hoodlum,--while Tim, the prize-fighter, was probably one of the friends of her family that the policeman had probably now under arrest down in that "corner house." Thrilling with this interpretation, Josie pulled at Lizzie's sleeve, and made a frantic appeal to her to come away as the policeman had advised, adding,--

"We are decent girls, and--it's a disgrace to have anything to do with such a lot as Becky and her family and--"

"What yer talkin' 'bout?" suddenly interrupted the policeman,--"what yer talkin' 'bout? Becky Hawkins a disgrace to yer! Come down here 'n' see what the Cove Street folks think of Becky Hawkins!" and he wheeled around as suddenly as he had spoken, and beckoned the girls to follow him.

They followed him down to the corner house, which stood blackened with smoke and water, but otherwise uninjured, for it was just here that the flames had been arrested, and in the hall-way the few poor remnants of the household goods that had been saved from the other tenements were huddled together. Pushing past these, the policeman stopped at an open door whence issued a sound of voices. Lizzie started forward as a familiar tone struck her ear, and smiling she exclaimed, "That's Becky!"

But the policeman pulled her back. "Wait a minute!" he said.

"Who's that speakin' to me?" called out the familiar voice. "Is it Lizzie Macdonald from the store?"

"Yes, yes!" and, the policeman no longer holding her back, Lizzie stepped over the threshold. There were two or three others in the room; but over and beyond them Lizzie caught sight of Becky's big black eyes, and hurrying forward cried: "Oh, Becky, I've only just got out of the store, and just read about the fire, and I thought mebbe you were hurt, and I came as fast as I could to see if I couldn't do something for you; but I'm so glad you are all right--But," coming nearer and finding that Becky was not standing, as she supposed, but propped up on a table, "you're *not* all right, are you?"

"No, I--I guess--I'm all wrong," responded Becky, with a queer little smile, and an odd quaver to her voice.

"Oh, Becky, Becky, they ought to have taken better care of you,--a little thing like you!"

"'Twas *she* was takin' care of other folks," spoke up one of the women in the room.

"Yes, 'twas a-savin' my Tim that did it," broke forth another. "She'd got down the stairs all safe, and then she thought o' Tim and ran back for him. She know'd I wasn't to home, and he was all alone; and she saved him for me,--she saved him for me! She helped him out onto the roof; 'twas too late for the stairs then, and a fire-man got him down the 'scape; but Becky--Becky was behind, and the fire follered so fast, she made a jump--and fell--oh, Becky! Becky!"

"Hush now!" said the other woman. "Don't keep a-goin' over it; yer worry her, and it's no use."

"Went back for Tim, saved Tim the prize-fighter!" thought Lizzie, in dumb amazement.

"The kid'll be all right soon," broke in another voice here.

Lizzie looked up, and saw a rough fellow, who had just come in, gazing down at Becky with an expression that strangely softened his hard face.

Becky lifted her eyes at the sound of the voice.

"Hello, Jake," she said faintly.

"Hello, Becky, yer'll be all right soon, won't yer?"

"I'm all right now," said Becky, sleepily, "and Tim's all right. He didn't get burnt, but the basket and all the pretty flowers did. If I could make another--"

"*I'll* make another for you," said Lizzie, pressing forward.

"And hang it for Tim?" asked Becky.

"Yes," answered Lizzie. Something in Lizzie's expression, in her tone, roused Becky's wandering memory, and with a sudden flash of her old mischief she said,--

"He's a fren' o' mine. Show up, Tim, and lemme interduce yer."

There was a movement on the other side of the table where Becky lay; and then Lizzie saw, struggling up from a chair, a tiny crippled body, wasted and shrunken,--the body of a child of seven with a shapely head and the face of an intelligent boy of fifteen.

"That's him,--that's Tim,--the fightin' gen'leman I tole yer 'bout," said Becky, with a gay little smile at the remembrance of her joke and how she "played it on 'em," and at the look of astonishment now on Lizzie's face. And still with the gay little smile, but fainter voice,--

"Yer'll tell 'em, Lizzie,--the girls in the store,--how I played it on 'em; and when I git back--I'll--"

"Give her some air; she's faint," cried one of the women.

The tall young rough, Jake, sprang to the window and pulled it open, letting in a fresh wind that blew straight up from the grassy banks beyond the Cove.

"Do yer feel better, Becky?" he asked, as he saw her face brighten.

"I--I feel fus' rate--all well, Jake, and--I--I smell the Mayflowers. They warn't burnt, were they? And oh, ain't they jolly, ain't they jolly! Tim, Tim!"

"Yes, yes, Becky," answered Tim, in a shaking voice.

"Wait for me here Tim,--I--I'm goin' to find 'em for yer, Tim,--ther, ther Mayflowers. They're close by; don't yer smell 'em? Close by--I'm goin'--to find 'em for yer, Tim!" And with a radiant smile of anticipation Becky's soul went out upon its happy quest, leaving behind her the grime and poverty of Cove Street forever.

The two women--and one of them was Becky's aunt with whom the girl had always lived--broke into sobs and tears; but as the latter looked at the radiant face, she said suddenly,--

"She's well out of it all."

"But there's them that'll be worse for her goin'," said the other; "and 't ain't only Tim I mean, it's the like o' *him*," nodding towards Jake, who was slipping quietly out of the room,--"it's the like o' him. They looked up to her, they did,--bit of a thing as she was. She was that straight and plucky and gin'rous she did 'em good; she made 'em better. Jake's often said she was the Cove Street mascot."

And with these words sounding in her ears, Lizzie crept softly from the room. Just over the threshold, in the shadow of the broken bits of furniture that had been saved from the fire, she started to see Matty and Josie still waiting for her.

"What!" she cried, "have you been here all the time--have you seen--have you heard--"

They nodded; and Matty whispered brokenly,--

"Oh, Lizzie, I ain't never again goin' to think bad things of anybody I don't know."

"Nor I, nor I," said Josie, huskily.

ALLY.
CHAPTER I.

"What have you done with those new overshoes, Ally?"

"Put 'em away."

"Well, you can just go and get 'em, then. Come, hurry up, for I want to wear 'em down town."

But Ally didn't move.

"Ally, do you hear?" cried her cousin Florence.

"Yes, I hear, but I ain't a-going to mind you. The rubbers are mine, and you've worn 'em about enough already; you're stretching 'em all out, for your foot is bigger than mine."

"No such thing. I'm not hurting them in the least."

"Yes, you are; and you are taking the gloss all off 'em, too, and I want 'em to look new when I wear 'em in Boston."

"Well, I never heard of such selfish, stingy meanness as this. It's raining hard, and you'd let me go out and get my feet sopping wet rather than lend me your new rubbers."

"Why don't you wear your own old ones?"

"Because they leak."

"They've leaked ever since I got this new pair!" retorted Ally, scornfully. "But it isn't these rubbers only; you're always borrowing my things. There's my blue jacket; you've worn it till the edge is threadbare, and you've worn my brown hat until it looks as shabby--and--there! you've got my silver bangle on now! You're no better than a thief, Florence Fleming!"

"A thief! that's a nice pretty thing to say to *me*! I should like to know who buys your things for you? Isn't it *my father* and Uncle John? I should like to know where you'd be, Alice Fleming, if it wasn't for Uncle John and father. Here, take your old bangle and keep it, and everything else that you've got. I never want to see anything of yours again; and I'm glad you're going off to Boston to Uncle John's for the rest of the winter, and I wish you'd stay there and never come back here,--I do!"

"I wish so too. Nobody in Uncle John's family would ever be so mean as to fling it in my face that I was a poor little beggar of an orphan."

"Uncle John's family! Uncle John's wife said the last time she was here that she dreaded the winter on your account,--there!"

"Aunt Kate--said that?"

"Yes, she did; I heard her."

A strange look came into Ally's eyes, and all the pretty color faded from her cheeks, as she cried out in a hoarse, passionate voice,--

"You're a cruel, bad girl, Florence Fleming, and I hope some day you'll have something cruel and bad come to you to punish you!" and with these words the excited child flung herself across her little bed, and burst into a paroxysm of stormy sobs and tears.

"Here, here, what's the matter now?" called out Mrs. Fleming, Florence's mother, coming across the hall and pushing the bedroom door open.

"Ask Ally," answered Florence, coolly,--so coolly, so calmly, that it was quite natural to suppose that she was much less to blame in the present disturbance than her cousin; and as poor Ally was past speaking, Florence had a double advantage, and Mrs. Fleming, glancing from one girl to the other, thought she understood the situation perfectly, and in consequence said rather sharply,--

"I do wish, Ally, you would try to control your temper a little more!" and with these words the lady turned and left the room, her daughter Florence following her. As they crossed the hall, Ally unfortunately overheard her aunt say to Florence, "I am thankful that you two are to be separated to-morrow for the rest of the winter. I hope by spring some other arrangement can be made to keep you apart. We shall never have any peace while--"

The rest of the sentence was lost to Ally. But she was quite sure it was--"while Ally is with us;" and a fresh gust of stormy sobs and tears shook the child's frame, as she thus concluded the sentence. A fresh gust also of stormy resentment and self-pity shook the girl. "Oh, yes, it's always Ally, always Ally, that's to blame," she said to herself. "It would be very different if I wasn't a poor little beggar of an orphan; yes, indeed, very different. If I was a *rich* orphan, if papa and mamma had left a lot of money to be taken care of with me, I guess things would be different,--I guess they would. I guess Florence Fleming and her mother wouldn't lay everything that goes wrong to *me* then, and I guess Aunt Kate wouldn't say that she dreaded the winter on account of me,--no, I guess she wouldn't! Oh, oh!" with a fresh sob, "I wish some other arrangement *could* be made away from 'em all. They don't any of 'em want me, not any of 'em, and I'd rather go to an orphan asylum. I'd rather--I'd rather--oh, I'd rather go to *jail* than to *them*!" and down into the pillow again went the fuzzy yellow head of this little hot-tempered Ally Fleming, who called herself so pityingly "a poor little beggar of an orphan."

The facts of the case were these: Ally's father and mother had both died when she was seven years old, leaving her to the care of her two nearest relatives,--her father's two brothers,--Mr. Tom and Mr. John Fleming. As her father had little or nothing to leave her, he had requested that the burden of her maintenance should be equally divided between the uncles, the child to live alternately with each family, six months with one and six with the other. She had been old enough when she was thus transplanted from her own home to realize more or less the peculiar condition of things; and as she was quick-tempered and sensitive, she very soon began to take note of any comment or remark regarding herself that was dropped in her hearing, and very often misunderstood or made too much of it. But there was no denying, whichever way you looked at it, that it was rather a difficult situation for both sides, and that the Fleming aunts and uncles and cousins had something to put up with, as well as Ally. But that Ally was the most to be pitied there was also no denying, for she could remember with unfading vividness being the centre of love, the one special darling in *one* home, and now she hadn't even one home, and was nobody's darling. As she lay there on the bed shaken by her sobs, she pictured to herself, as she had pictured many, many times in these three years, the happy home that she had lost. For three years this once petted child had been learning what it was to be one of many, or, as she herself put it, one *too* many.

CHAPTER II.

The next day at noon Ally was on her way to Boston, where she was to live for the next six months in her uncle John's family. Both her uncle Tom and his wife,

Aunt Ann, had gone to the station to see her off, and both of them had kissed her good-by, and given her various messages to deliver to the Boston relations. Everything was going on as pleasantly as possible until Aunt Ann at the very last stooped down and said,--

"Now, try, Ally, try while you are with your aunt Kate to control your temper. You mustn't fly up at every little thing, and expect to have your own way with everybody. It is very difficult to live with people who act like that, and nobody can love them. Remember that, Ally;" and with these words, Mrs. Fleming bent still lower to touch Ally's lips with a final farewell kiss. But Ally at this movement turned suddenly, and the kiss that was meant for her lips fell upon her cheek.

"Such an uncomfortable disposition as that child has, I never met before, never!" ejaculated Mrs. Fleming, as she joined her husband outside the car.

"What's she done now?" asked Uncle Tom.

His wife described the girl's swift evasive movement away from her.

Uncle Tom laughed, and then sighed. "Poor little soul," he said; "she's going to have a hard time of it in life, I'm afraid."

"She's going to make those who live with her have a hard time," answered Aunt Ann, resentfully thinking of her rejected kiss.

"'Mustn't fly up at every little thing!'" repeated Ally to herself, as she was left alone in her seat. "She'd better give Florence some of her good advice. She'd better tell her not to aggravate folks 'most to death, and then stand off so cool, and make everybody else seem in the wrong. Hard to live with! Mebbe I *am* hard to live with; but I don't play double like that; and as for nobody's loving me, these relations of mine never loved me--any of 'em--from the first."

As Ally came to this conclusion in her thought, she happened to look out of the car window, and there, why, there was her aunt Ann and uncle Tom outside on the platform, standing at another car window farther down, talking and laughing in the liveliest manner with some friends they had met. Uncle Tom didn't seem in the least haste now, and ever so many minutes ago he had said to her, "Well, good-by, Ally!" and rushed off as if there wasn't another minute to spare,--not another minute; and here was a gentleman in front of her, saying to a friend of his at that very instant, "There's plenty of time; it's ten minutes before the cars start;" and then she heard a lady say to another lady, "There's no need of my leaving you yet; we've got oceans of time;" and all about her, Ally now noticed various groups of friends and relations lingering lovingly together until the last moment; and noting all this, a bitter little look came into Miss Ally's face, and a bitter little thought came into her heart,--a thought that said tauntingly, "There, this shows you, Ally Fleming, what kind of relations you've got; this shows you how much they care for you!"

And by and by, as the cars started up and sped along, this bitter little thought also sped along, carrying in its wake all the bitter little thoughts of yesterday and to-day. Ally was quite accustomed to travelling by herself on this trip to and from New York. It was a perfectly simple thing to sit in the car-seat where she had been placed by one uncle, until at the end of the trip she was met by the other uncle, and taken charge of,--a perfectly simple, easy matter, and Ally had heretofore quite enjoyed it; but now, looking about her, and seeing the groups of other people's relations going home to Thanksgiving, she began to think it was a very lonesome thing to be travelling all alone by herself; and just as this occurred to her, what should happen but that one of these groups should turn inquisitively to her and ask, "Are you travelling all by yourself, little girl?" and when Ally had answered, "Yes," this inquisitive person commented upon her being such a little girl to travel all by herself; and then, when Ally told her rather proudly that she was ten years old, the inquisitive person had said, "Well, I don't know what *my* little ten-year-old girl would think to be sent off to travel all alone. I shall tell her when I get home what a brave little girl I met."

Ally thought all this was said out of pity and wonder, and that the lady thought her very much neglected and forlorn. But instead of that, the lady meant only to praise and compliment her; and thus, in this way and that way, the bitter little thoughts kept growing and growing, as the cars sped on, until long before the end of her journey came, poor Ally felt that there never was a much more friendless girl than she was; and when the cars steamed into the Boston station, she said to herself, "I wonder if Uncle John is dreading the winter on my account, as Aunt Kate is?" and with this thought she stepped out on the platform. But where *was* Uncle John? She expected to see him at once, coming forward to lift her from the steps. Where *was* he now? and Ally looked at the faces before her with wondering scrutiny. She jumped down--for people were pressing behind her--and moved on, scanning the face of every gentleman she saw with anxious eyes. No one of them, however, was that of Uncle John. What *was* the matter? Didn't he know the train she was to take? Of course he did, for Uncle Tom had told her that he had telegraphed that he would meet her at the Boston station at five o'clock. Of course he knew, so he must have forgotten her. Yes, that was it,--he had forgotten all about her! Ally was not a specially timid child; but as she stood in the big station-building, and realized that there was not a soul she knew there to look out for her, a feeling of dismay overtook her. If it were in the morning or at noonday, it wouldn't have seemed so dreadful; but though the electric lights flashed everything into brilliance, it was a November day, and half-past five o'clock was after nightfall. What *should* she do? There was no sign of Uncle John, and the passengers who had arrived with her were fast disappearing. Very soon the people in the station would begin to notice her, to ask questions, and then perhaps some police-officer would take her to the police-station, as a lost child. She'd heard that that was what they always did. It was just as this thought came into her head that she caught sight of one of those very big burly blue-coated individuals. He had his hand on the collar of a boy about her own age, and she heard him say to him in a big burly voice,--

"What yer hangin' 'round here for? Lost, eh? That's a likely story. Come, off with yer, if yer don't want ter be locked up!"

Poor little Ally didn't stop to reason,--to think of the difference in the outward appearance of herself and the boy,--to see that the policeman knew the boy perfectly well for a mischievous young scamp who was up to no good. She didn't stop to consider anything; but with those words, "If yer don't want ter be locked up," ringing in her ears, she turned and ran from the station-building as fast as her legs could carry her. As she came out upon the sidewalk, she saw the colored lights of a street car. Oh, joy, it was the very up-town car that would take her close to Beacon Street! But oh, horror! She suddenly recollected that Uncle John no longer lived on Beacon Street. He had moved last month into a new house on Marlborough Street, and oh, what *was* the number? She "had heard Uncle Tom read it from a letter. It had a lot of 9's in it. Nine hundred and--why--99--999, three 9's; yes, yes, that was it;" and with this conviction, Ally gave a hop skip and a jump into the car, just as it was about to start off, for this very car she knew would take her nearer to Marlborough Street than to Beacon Street. Her spirits rose as she felt herself carried along; and in due time she found the three 9's, and tripped up the steps of the house in

Marlborough Street bearing that number. Her heart beat very fast with a sense of relief and injury, mixed with a certain elation at her own enterprise, as she rang the bell. Wouldn't they be surprised, and wouldn't Uncle John--But some one opening the door scattered her questioning thoughts; and--why, who was this somebody? It must be a new servant with the new house, and a manservant too. Uncle John must be getting better off,--they had had only two maids before. It never entered Ally's head to ask the strange servant if Mr. Fleming lived there. Why should she ask what she was so sure of? She simply asked, "Where's Uncle John and Aunt Kate and the rest of them?"

The man looked bewildered, and repeated, "Uncle John?"

"Yes, Uncle John and Aunt Kate. I'm Ally, and Uncle John telegraphed that he would meet me at the five-o'clock train, and he wasn't there, and I came up all alone. Where are they? In the parlor?" and Ally stepped in over the threshold.

"I guess there's some mistake," said the man; "I guess your uncle John--"

"No, there wasn't any mistake, for he telegraphed to Uncle Tom. He must have forgotten."

"But your uncle doesn't--"

"What is it, James? What is wanted?" interrupted some one here. The "some one" was a big, tall gentleman coming down the stairs, whom Ally, as she looked up in the rather confusing half light of the lower hall, at once took for her uncle, and rushing forward she ran up to meet him, crying,--

"Oh, Uncle John! Uncle John! I was so scared not to find you at the station, and I came up here all alone on the street car!"

But in the very next instant she started back and gasped: "But--but it isn't--you're not--you're not Uncle John! Where is he, oh, where is he?"

"You've made a mistake, my little girl!" exclaimed the gentleman,--"a mistake in the house. This isn't your uncle John's, but--"

"Not Uncle John's? Why--why--this is 999!" interrupted Ally, tremulously.

"Yes; but--"

"Oh! oh!" cried poor Ally, as a fresh flash of memory overcame her, "that must be the--the--" She was going to say, "the old Beacon Street number," when, confused and dismayed, she gave another step backward, her foot slipped, and she fell headlong to the foot of the stairs, where she lay white and motionless, not a sigh or moan escaping her as she was lifted and carried into the parlor.

CHAPTER III.

The sun was shining brightly into the pretty new dining-room on Marlborough Street where Uncle John lived, and swinging in its beams a great gray parrot named Peter kept calling out, "Ally's come, Ally's come! give her a kiss! give her a kiss!"

The room was empty when the parrot began; but presently Uncle John and Aunt Kate came in. At sight of them the parrot screamed, "Hello! hello!" and then repeated louder than ever, "Ally's come! Ally's come! give her a kiss! give her a kiss!"

"For pity's sake, put the bird out!" exclaimed Uncle John. "I can't stand *that now*!"

"Yes, put him out, do!" said Aunt Kate to the servant who was just then bringing in the coffee.

In a few moments the three daughters of the family--Laura and Maud and Mary--appeared.

"Have you heard anything about her this morning?" asked the eldest,--Laura,--as she took her seat at table.

Uncle John shook his head.

"And the police haven't got a clew yet?"

"No, nor the detectives."

"What I *can't* understand is why she didn't wait in the ladies' room until you came, papa. She might have known you *would* come *sometime*."

"We don't know yet that she got as far as Boston," said Mrs. Fleming.

"Why, Uncle Tom's telegram in answer to papa's that he saw her off on the 11.30 train proves that."

"It doesn't prove that she came through to Boston."

"'Came through'! Why, upon earth, should she leave the cars before she reached Boston?"

"She might have made the acquaintance of some young people, and stepped off at a restaurant station with them to buy fruit, and so got left."

"But she would have taken a later train then, and papa has been to the later ones."

"Don't--don't wonder and speculate any more why a little girl of ten years didn't do exactly as a grown-up person would have done," burst forth Uncle John. "The whole blame lies with us, or with Tom and me. We should never have allowed such a child to be sent off alone like that."

"But, papa, it isn't an uncommon thing for a child of her age to travel like that."

"It isn't very *common*, and it ought not to be."

"Maybe she's run away," suddenly exclaimed the youngest of the daughters,--a girl of fourteen.

"Mary!" cried the other two; and "How can you make fun like that *now*?" said Mrs. Fleming, reprovingly.

"I didn't say it to make fun," protested Mary,--"I didn't, truly; but--but Ally was very queer sometimes. She took up everything so, and got offended, or thought you didn't care for her. One day I asked her why she didn't take things as *I* did,--spat, and forget it the next minute, and she said, 'Because I'm not like you, *I only happened here*'! Wasn't that droll?"

"Droll!" exclaimed Uncle John. "I think it's the most pathetic thing I ever heard. What have we all been doing that she should feel like this?"

"But she liked being *here* better than at Uncle Tom's. Florence was always tormenting her one way and another."

"The trouble with her is that she was an only child, and, transplanted suddenly into two large families, she couldn't fit herself to the new circumstances," said Mrs. Fleming.

"And the trouble with *us* has been," spoke up Uncle John, "that we didn't take that fact into consideration enough, and try to help her to fit into the new circumstances. Poor little soul, if we ever get her back again--"

"Oh, don't, don't talk like that,--'if we ever get her back again!' as if she were a Charley Ross child that had been kidnapped," burst forth Mary, with a breaking voice. "*I* meant to be good to Ally, and that's why I taught Peter to say, 'Ally's come, Ally's come! give her a kiss! give her a kiss!' I thought it would be such a pretty welcome, and Ally'd be so pleased, she'd believe we *did* care for her when she heard that."

"You're a little trump, Mary," declared her father, with a suspicious moisture in his eyes. "I only hope if--*when* Ally comes back--But, hark, there's the door-bell!" as a sharp peal rang through the house. "It may be one of the detectives."

"A gentleman to see you in the parlor, sir," said the maid a moment later, as she brought in a card.

Uncle John glanced at the card, and then, uttering an exclamation of surprise, passed it over to his wife, and, jumping up hastily, left the room.

"Is it the chief of the detectives?" asked Laura, animatedly.

"It isn't a detective at all; it's Dr. Phillips."

"You don't mean *the* Dr. Phillips,--*Bernard* Phillips?"

"Yes."

"How strange, and at this hour in the morning! It must be something about Thanksgiving exercises," interposed Maud.

"But we're not *his* parishioners. We don't go to *his* church!"

"Oh, dear!" cried Mary; "I'm *so* disappointed. I did hope it was the detective bringing Ally back."

"Kate!" called Uncle John's voice here, "will you come into the parlor?" and Mrs. Fleming, obeying this call, found herself a minute after exchanging greetings with the unexpected visitor.

"I want you to tell her, Doctor, just what you've told me exactly," said Uncle John. "It's about Ally, my dear," to his wife. "She's found, and--and--"

"She is at my house," took up the Doctor; and then he told of the little girl who had come to his house the night before, of her grievous disappointment, and the accident that had befallen her,--an accident that had robbed her of consciousness for a time, and from which she had only sufficiently recovered within the last few hours to answer the questions that were put to her in regard to her relations, that steps might be taken to restore her to them.

"And she is seriously hurt,--she couldn't come with you?" broke in Aunt Kate, breathlessly.

"No, she was not seriously hurt," he assured her; and then came that most delicate and difficult part of the Doctor's task,--to tell, in what gentle phrase he could, that this wilful child refused to accompany him; that she had taken a foolish fancy into her head that her relations did not care for her,--a fancy that had been strengthened into positive belief when she failed to find her uncle at the station, and had suggested to her a wild little plan of going away from them altogether, into some orphans' home that she had heard of, where she was sure a place could be found for her. Very gentle, indeed, was the phrasing of all this,--so gentle and full of sweet human consideration for everybody's shortcomings and mistakes that Aunt Kate forgot that the Doctor was a stranger; and with this forgetfulness the sharp pang of humiliation at a stranger's knowledge of such a family difficulty, and the little sting of resentment at Ally's attitude towards them all, was overborne to such an extent that she could frankly admit that her husband was right, and that none of them had had love and patience enough to help the child to fit into the new circumstances of her life.

It was an added pang, but there was no resentment in it, when she saw Ally's sudden shrinking from her as she entered the Doctor's parlor with him a little later.

To think that they had, though unwittingly, hurt and estranged the child like this, was Mrs. Fleming's first thought; and the tears came to her eyes, and her voice broke as she cried impulsively, "Oh, my little girl, my little girl!"

Ally started at the sight of these tears, at the sound of this tenderly breaking voice. And there was Uncle John; and *he* was crying too, and *his* voice was breaking as he said something. What was it he was saying?--that it was not forgetfulness, it was not neglect of her, that had made him fail to meet her at the station, but an untoward accident to the streetcar he was in that had delayed him. And what was that Aunt Kate was saying? That they *did* care for her, that they *did* want her, and that they had set the telegraphic wires all over the country to hunt for her and bring her back to them.

"But--but--Florence told me," faltered Ally, "that you dreaded the winter on my account,--I was so--so bad-tempered--so hard to live with."

"Dreaded the winter on your account! Florence told you I said that?" cried Mrs. Fleming, in amazement.

"She said she heard you say it to her mother."

A light broke over Mrs. Fleming's face. "Oh, I remember now perfectly. It was just after you were so ill with that bad throat, and I was speaking to your aunt

Ann about it, and I said to her, 'I dread the winter on Ally's account.' How could--how **could** Florence put such a mischievous meaning to my words?"

"Perhaps she only heard just those words," replied Ally, who would never take advantage of anybody.

"But why should she want to tell you what would hurt you like that?"

"We'd been quarrelling," answered Ally, with an honest brevity that was very edifying.

"But, as you see now it was for your bad throat, and not for your bad temper, that I dreaded the winter," said Aunt Kate, with a smile, "you will come back with us, and let us both try again. We meant to be good to you, dear; but we did not think enough that you had been unused to a big family,--that you were a little ewe lamb that had been transplanted into a great crowded fold, and left to find your place with the crowd; and you misunderstood this, and took us too hardly; but we're going to do better. We're going to be more thoughtful of one another, and you'll come home with us now, and we'll have our Thanksgiving dinner together, won't we?"

Childish and ignorant of the world's ways, as her wild idea in regard to her right to a place in an orphans' home proved her, Ally had a great deal of sense in other directions, and she began to perceive that she had not been the wilfully neglected and abused person she had thought herself, and to think, too, that perhaps Aunt Kate **might** have had something to bear from **her**. At any rate, her good sense made her see that her aunt had come to her with kind and generous intentions, and that the least she could do was to respond with what grace was in her power; and so with a little smile that had something pathetic in it to those who saw it, it was so tremulous with that pitiful doubt that had been born of the last three unhappy years, she put her hand into Mrs. Fleming's, and signified her readiness to go with her. And then and there, as she met that smile, Kate Fleming vowed to herself that never again through fault of hers should this child suffer for lack of loving care; and with this resolve warm in her heart, she clasped the little hand in hers more closely, and said brightly,--

"You'll see how glad the girls will be to see you, Ally, when we get home."

But Ally had no response to make to this. A great dread had seized her as she felt herself going to meet them. Uncle John's and Aunt Kate's assurance of regard was one thing, but Uncle John and Aunt Kate were not the girls, and poor Ally was quite sure that no one of them had ever cared very much for her, though Mary had alternately petted and laughed at her, and now--why, now, they might dislike her for making such a fuss, for Laura had often said she did dislike people so who made a fuss, and Maud would agree with Laura, and Mary would laugh at her more than ever. Oh, dear! oh, dear! if she could only go back! if she could only get that dear good Doctor to find her a place in--But, "Here we are, Ally!" said Uncle John; and "Here she is!" exclaimed three girlish voices; and there, standing in the doorway, were Laura and Maud and Mary; and at sight of their faces, at sound of their voices, Ally's dread began to vanish. And then, just then, it was that Peter, who had been banished to the hall, called out uproariously, "Ally's come! Ally's come! give her a kiss! give her a kiss!" and Mary called out after him, "I taught him to say that; I taught him more 'n a month ago."

"'More 'n a month ago'! Oh!" breathed Ally under her breath, "she liked me well enough for this *more 'n a month ago*!"

Uncle John and Aunt Kate and Laura and Maud and Mary were looking on, and they knew what Ally was thinking of,--the very words of it,--by that sudden radiant smile upon her face; and Mary was so pleased thereat, she had to cry out,--

"Oh, what a jolly Thanksgiving this is! Could anything be added to make it jollier?"

But something *was* added. When they were all at the dinner-table that night,--mother and father and girls and the three boys who had just come up from their boarding-school that very morning,--this telegram was brought in from Uncle Tom,--

"Thanks for word of Ally's safety. All send love. Florence is writing to her."

Ally's eyes opened wide with astonishment at this conclusion. Florence! Aunt Kate read the meaning of that astonished look, and sent a glance to Ally that said as plainly as *words* could say, "You see, even Florence didn't mean as badly as you thought."

AN APRIL FOOL.
CHAPTER I.

"Have you written it, Nelly?"

"Yes, I have it here in my pocket. I'll show it to you when I get a chance."

"Oh, show it now! There's as good a chance now as you'll have, for the rest of the girls are all on the other side of the room. Come;" and Lizzy Ryder held out her hand coaxingly.

Nelly sent a quick glance around the school-room, and then took from her pocket a small square envelope. The envelope was directed to Miss Angela Jocelyn. Lizzy Ryder gave a little giggle as she read this name; but as she drew forth the note-sheet and read written upon it in a slender pointed handwriting, "Miss Marian Selwyn requests the pleasure of Miss Angela Jocelyn's company on the evening of April 1st," her giggle became a smothered shriek, and she said to her cousin,--

"Oh, Nelly, it's perfect; she'll never suspect. It looks just like Marian Selwyn's writing. Wouldn't it be too good if we could somehow get hold of Angela's acceptance and keep it back, and have her actually *go* to the party. What *do* you suppose Marian would say to her when she walked in?"

"She wouldn't *say* anything, but she'd *look* so astonished, and she'd be so stiff that Miss Angela would very soon find out she wasn't very welcome. But we can't keep back the note very well, even if we could get hold of it,--it might get us into trouble, for it would be against the law; but there's no law against an April Fool letter of our own, and 'twill be just as good fun in the end, for Marian Selwyn, of course, will set Miss Angela right in double quick time after she receives her note. Oh, I can just imagine the top-lofty style in which she will inform Miss Angela that there must be some mistake."

"And then, of course, they'll both find out that somebody's been April-fooling them."

"Of course. But that isn't going to interfere with our fun. Miss Angela will be set down by that time just where I want her, when she discovers that her invitation is nothing but an April fool on her. I wish--But, hush, somebody's coming this way;" and in an instant Nelly had whisked into her pocket the note she had written, and the cousins were walking down the room, talking in a loud tone about their lessons. The "somebody coming" was a very quiet but a very observing girl, who, as she saw the sudden start of Lizzy and Nelly, also caught sight of the little white missive as it was whisked into Nelly's pocket, and immediately thought,--

"There's some mischief going on. I wonder what it is."

"That sly Mary Marcy, she's always spying 'round," whispered Nelly to her companion, as they passed along. Then in a high voice, thinking to mislead Mary, she cried, "Oh, Lizzy, now I've shown you *my* composition you must show me yours."

Mary Marcy was a shrewd girl as well as an observant one, and she laughed in her sleeve as she heard this.

"Composition! that was no school composition", she said to herself; and when a few minutes later the bell rang for the close of recess, and she saw Nelly send a significant glance to Lizzy as the two hurried to their seats, this shrewd, observant Mary was surer than ever that there was mischief going on, and when she went home that afternoon she told her mother what she had seen and heard, and how she felt about it,--for Mary was very confidential with her mother, and told her most of her school secrets. Mrs. Marcy listened to this telling with that placid Quaker way of hers, and remarked in her quaint Quaker phrase, "Thee mustn't be too suspicious, my dear; it maybe harmless mischief, after all." And then Mary had replied, "I shouldn't be suspicious of any of the other girls, mother; but Lizzy and Nelly Ryder are always doing and saying the mischievous things that have a sting in them;" and Mrs. Marcy, spite of her Quaker charity, then admitted that she had never quite liked the ways of those girls, and had often been sorry that they were in the Westboro' High School; "but, poor things," she added the moment she had made this admission, "they are more to be pitied than the persons they hurt, for *they* can get over the hurt, but these poor girls can't get over their own wrong-doing so easily. It makes a black mark on them every time, and black marks are hard to rub off; and thee'll see if they are up to any wrong-doing now, it will leave a mark, and so they'll get the worst of it in the long run."

"But it's always *such* a long run before a mark of that kind shows," laughed

Mary. "Girls of that sort seem to succeed in making everybody but themselves uncomfortable, and these two specially always appear to be so gay and full of good times with their giggle and chatter."

"But the Bible says, Mary, 'for as the crackling of thorns under a pot, so is the laughter of the fool;' and thee can think of this the next time thee hears the chatter, and then thee can say to thyself, 'It *may* be nothing but foolish folly, after all.'"

"Yes, it *may* be nothing but that," Mary allowed; but when the next morning she heard it again, her first doubts and suspicions returned in full force, and she said to herself, "I'm perfectly sure that there's something more than mere foolishness in this crackling of thorns. I'm perfectly sure there's mischief with a sting in it. I feel it in the air, and I'm just going to watch out and see if I can't stop it as I did that horrid St. Valentine business last winter."

And while good kind Mary was thus "watching out" for this mischief, there, only two or three seats away from her, sat Angela Jocelyn, about whom all the mischief was gathering as a dark cloud gathers over a fair sky. And Angela's sky was particularly fair to her just then, for she had been made very happy by the invitation she had received that morning,--so happy that she had said to her elder sister, Martha Jocelyn, "To think of Marian Selwyn's inviting *me*. Isn't it beautiful of her?" and Martha had answered back rather tartly, "I don't see why you should put such an emphasis on 'me,' as if you were so inferior. You're as good as Marian Selwyn."

"Yes, Martha, I know--it isn't that I feel inferior in--in myself," Angela exclaimed; "but the Selwyns have always had money and everything--always, and we are poor and have lived so out of the way that I say it's beautiful and kind of Marian, when she knows me so little. Why, Martha, I never see her anywhere but on the street and at Sunday-school."

"Well, she likes you, I suppose. She's taken a fancy to you, and she's independent enough, I should hope, to invite any girl she likes, if the girl *is* poor and lives out of the way," was Martha's cool reply.

Liked her! Taken a fancy to her! How Angela's heart jumped at this suggestion! Could it be possible that this lovely fortunate Marian Selwyn, that she had always admired from afar off, had taken a fancy to *her*,--poor, plain little Angela Jocelyn,--was her thought. And it was with this thought quickening her pulses that she wrote a cordial acceptance to the note of invitation; and it was this thought that sent such a bright look into her face that morning, that Mary Marcy said to her friend and seat-mate, Anna Richards, "Look at Angela Jocelyn, she is really growing pretty;" and a little later at the recess that followed directly after a recitation where Angela had easily led, as usual, Mary, catching sight of the frowning faces of Lizzy and Nelly Ryder, exclaimed: "Anna, if Angela Jocelyn is going to add good looks to her braininess, those Ryder girls will be more jealous of her than ever."

"And they pretend to look down on Angela because she is poor and her mother and sister take in sewing," responded Anna.

"All the same they don't look down on what Angela really *is*. She is superior to them in brains, and they know it, and that makes them want to pull her down," answered Mary.

"Yes, I heard Nelly Ryder say last week that Angela was altogether too conceited, and ought to be 'taken down'; and it would be just like Nelly Ryder to try to do it sometime."

"*Sometime*! I believe she is trying to do it now. I believe that that is the mischief she and her cousin Lizzy are planning this moment," cried Mary.

"What *do* you mean?"

"I'll tell you;" and Mary related, as she had related to her mother, what she had seen and heard.

"Nelly Ryder has never forgiven Angela for getting the history prize; Nelly thought herself sure of it,--she as good as told me so," was Anna's only remark upon this.

"And now she's going to play some trick on Angela to take her down, as she calls it; that's what you think, isn't it? And that's what *I* think. Oh, Anna, I wish I could ferret out the mischief and stop it. It will be something hateful and mortifying to poor Angela, I know. If I could only get some clew to what it is, so as to warn her."

"Yes; but as we are not sure that there *is* any mischief, after all, you mustn't say anything to anybody yet."

"No, of course not; but I'll keep a sharp lookout, and I *may* hear or see something that will give me a hint. What fun it would be to outwit one of the Ryder schemes!"

"Mary! with all your Quaker bringing-up, I do believe you are just pining for what our Jack would call 'a scrimmage.'"

"Well, I am, if that means getting the better of mischief-makers," Mary confessed with a laugh.

"But you won't succeed, if the mischief-makers are Nelly and Lizzy Ryder, Those, girls seem to get the best of everything and everybody. Think now, for one thing, of their being acquaintances of Marian Selwyn's, and invited to her birthday party!"

"Oh, well, that is family acquaintance, Anna. The Ryders have always known the Selwyns, just as we have. The Selwyns and Ryders and Marcys have lived in Westboro', and visited each other for ages."

"I wish *I* had, and then I might have been invited to this wonderful birthday party," exclaimed Anna, with a certain earnestness of tone that belied her gay little laugh, and made Mary say regretfully,--

"I wish I'd known you felt like this last week, I would have had you and Marian 'round to tea, and then you would have got acquainted, and she'd have been sure to have invited you; but it's too late now, for the party comes off Thursday, you know."

"Thursday! Why, Thursday is the first of April.. How funny that one's birthday should come on the first of April!"

"Funny--why?"

"Why? Because it's April-fool's day."

"Oh, I see; but I'm so used to Marian's birthdays, I don't always stop to think of that."

"But don't some people think of it? Don't they sometimes play--Oh, oh, Mary, Mary, mayn't this be your clew? Don't you believe that Nelly Ryder has been planning an April-fool trick upon Angela in connection with this party?"

Mary, who had been sitting on one of the wide window-seats in the recitation-room, jumped to her feet at this, with a little scream of: "Oh, Anna, you've hit it. I do believe it *is* the clew. Why *didn't* I think of April-fool's day,--that it would be just the opportunity Nelly Ryder would take advantage of to play a trick, because she could throw it off from herself as a mere April joke, if her hand was found out in it. Yes, yes, she has planned to drag Angela into some performance or other on the birthday that will make her ridiculous and offensive to Marian,--sending her on some fool's errand to Marian, perhaps the night of the party, as somebody sent poor little Tilly Drake last year with a silly message to Clara Harrington that made Clara furious, and mortified Tilly dreadfully."

"Oh, well, Angela wouldn't be taken in like that; she's brighter than Tilly."

"Angela is just the one to be taken in. She's one of the brightest persons I ever saw about books and things of that kind, but she is very innocent and unsuspecting. Anna, I'll tell you what I'm going to do. I'm going to see Marian this noon, and I'm going to tell her what I suspect."

"No, I wouldn't do that; it wouldn't be fair, for it's only our suspicion, and we *may* be on the wrong track altogether."

"But what am I to do? Sit still and let some horrid thing perhaps go on that I might stop?"

"I'll tell you what you might do. You might say to Marian that you had got an idea that somebody was going to play a trick on her birthday,--upon her and some unsuspecting person; that you didn't know *what* the trick was to be, and you might be all wrong in your suspicion that there was to be one, but you thought that you ought to put her on her guard. You might say this to her without mentioning a name."

"Oh, Anna, Anna, what a cautious little thing you are with your 'mays' and your 'mights;' but you are right, you are right, and I'll go to Marian this noon, and say just what you've told me to say, and not a word more."

CHAPTER II.

Mary thought it would be a very easy matter to say to Marian what Anna had suggested, but it wasn't so easy as she thought. Marian was a year older than herself, and that meant a good deal to a girl of fifteen,--a year older and more than a year beyond her, with the experience of Washington city life and schools during the winter months. In fact, to Mary, who had not seen her for the past few months, she appeared so experienced and grown-up, as she came into the room to meet her, that that young person felt all at once very young and awkward, and as a consequence made such a boggle of what she had to say, that Marian, entirely misunderstanding, exclaimed in amazement,--

"You want me to get up an April joke on my birthday, Mary? I couldn't think of such a thing; I hate April jokes."

"No, no, you misunderstand," burst forth Mary; and then, forgetting all her awkwardness, she made her little statement over again, and this time succinctly and clearly. And now it was *her* turn to be amazed; for before she had got entirely to the end of her statement, Marian starting up pulled a note from her pocket and cried, "Read this, Mary! read this!"

It was Angela's cordial note of acceptance.

"And she had no invitation from *me*. I never invited her, I scarcely knew her," went on Marian.

"She had no invitation from *you*, but she thought she had. It isn't Angela who is playing a trick upon *you*. Somebody has played a trick upon *her*,--has written in your name. Oh, don't you see? *She* is the innocent person I meant."

"But who--who is the guilty one,--the one who has *dared* to do this?" cried Marian.

"I can't tell you yet whom I think it is, because I haven't any proof, and it wouldn't be fair to call names unless I had sure proof."

"Well, look here. All my notes were sealed with my monogram seal, but I used a variety of colored wax. Everybody is interested in comparing seals now, and so can't you make an excuse to Angela that you want to compare the seals in the different colors, and borrow her note of invitation, and then bring it to me? If I could see that note, I might know the handwriting, and then I'd know who played this shabby, cruel trick. And I ought to know, that I mayn't suspect an innocent person."

"But the note that Angela received may not be sealed with wax."

"Oh, yes, it will. Whoever sent that note had seen mine, I am certain, and of course would use wax, as I did. Now, won't you do this little service for me, Mary?" urged Marian, entreatingly.

Mary laughed. "Yes, I'll do it," she answered, "though I'm not very clever at playing theatre. I've too much Quaker blood in me for that; but it's a good cause, and I'll do the best I can, and I'll do it now, for Angela's sure to be at home now;" and suiting her action to her word, Mary started off then and there upon her errand.

And so surely and swiftly did she do her best on this errand that Marian gave a little scream of surprise as she saw her coming back, and, "You've not got it already?" she cried, running to meet her.

"Yes, here it is. Angela gave it to me at once."

"Just the size of *my* paper, and the wax--you see I was right. There *is* wax, and a seal-stamp that looks like *my* stamp, but isn't," exclaimed Marian. "Now for the handwriting!" One glance at the address on the envelope; then, pulling out the note, she bent breathlessly over it for a moment. In another moment she was calling out triumphantly: "I know it! I know it! She tried to imitate mine, but I know these M's and r's and A's. They're Nelly Ryder's! they're Nelly Ryder's! Look here;" and running to her desk, the excited girl produced another note, and placed it beside the one that Angela had received. It was Nelly Ryder's acceptance of her invitation; and Mary, looking at the peculiar M's and r's and A's saw as clearly as Marian herself the proof of the same hand in each note.

"And I should know her 'hand' anywhere, for I've had hundreds of notes from her, first and last," Marian went on. "But to think of her playing such a trick as this! I never had any admiration for her, or her cousin either; but I *didn't* think either one of them could do such a mischievous, vulgar thing. But *you* did, Mary, for this is the girl you suspected."

"Yes, because I had known more of her than you had,--going to school with her every day;" and then Mary told what she had known, and what she had seen herself, winding up with, "But I didn't like to tell you all this before I had certain proof, for I wanted to be fair, you know."

"And you *have* been fair, more than fair; and now--"

"Well, go on, what do you stop for--now what?"

"Wait and see;" and Marian nodded her head, and compressed her lips into a firm, resolute line.

"Oh, Marian, are you going to punish Nelly?" cried Mary, a little alarmed at these indications.

Marian nodded again.

"Yes, I'm going to punish her."

"Oh, how, when, where?"

"When? On Thursday night. Where? At the birthday party. How? Wait and see."

CHAPTER III.

It was the evening of the first of April,--a beautiful, still, starry evening, with all the chill and frost of early spring blown out of it by the friendly winds of March, and all the lovely promises of summer buddings and flowerings wafting into it from waiting May and June.

A "just perfect evening," said more than one girl delightedly, as she set out arrayed in all her furbelows for the birthday party. A "just perfect evening." And no one said this more emphatically, and felt it more emphatically, than Mary Marcy and Angela Jocelyn,--Mary in her pretty and becoming if rather plain white gown of China silk, and Angela in her old white cambric that had been 'done over' for the hundredth time, perhaps, and was neither pretty nor becoming, with its skimp skirt and sleeves and shrunken waist. But a new gown had been out of the question just then with the Jocelyns, and Angela had to make the best of the old one; and it did not seem at all hard to make a very good 'best' of it, when she stood in her own little bedroom, with Martha tying the well-worn blue sash around the shrunken waist, and her mother looking on and saying, "It really looks very nice, and that sash *does* wash so well."

But when she went up into the great brilliantly lighted bedchamber at the Selwyns', and saw Mary Marcy in her perfectly fitting gown drawing on her delicate gloves, and talking with several young ladies beautifully dressed in fresh muslin and silk, the skimp skirt and sleeves, the shrunken waist and washed sash, seemed all at once very mean and shabby to Angela. They seemed still meaner and shabbier when two other girls appeared in yet prettier costumes of fresh daintiness; and when these two dropped their little hooded shoulder-wraps of silk and lace, and she saw that they were the two Ryder cousins, poor Angela suddenly began to feel a strange sense of awkwardness and unfitness. This feeling increased as she noticed the unmistakable start that the cousins gave as they caught sight of her, and heard Nelly's astonished exclamation, "What! *you* here?"

It was a bitter moment; but a bitterer was yet to come, when Lizzy Ryder, with that innocent little way of hers, said,--

"Oh, if you've come to help take our things off, ***do*** help me with this scarf, Angela!"

If Angela could but have known then and there that this was only a petty stab from one petty jealous girl! But she did not know. She heard the words, apparently so innocently spoken, and said to herself, "They think I am here as a servant, not as a guest!" and with a miserable confused feeling that everything was wrong, from her acceptance of the invitation to her shabby gown, she started back with all her confusion merging into one thought to get away out of the sight of these well-dressed happy girls. But as she started back, Mary Marcy, who had heard Lizzy Ryder's speech, started forward and called out: "Oh, Angela, how do you do? I didn't see you when you came in. I--I've been expecting to see you, though; and now shall we go down together?"

Angela couldn't speak. She could only give a little nod of assent, and yield herself to kind Mary's guidance, with a deep breath of relief. It was only a partial relief, however. She had yet to go down into the brilliant parlor with its crowd of Selwyn cousins, yet to face, in that old shrunken gown with its washed sash, all those critical eyes. Oh, what if all those eyes should look at her with a stare of astonishment, such as Lizzy and Nelly Ryder had bestowed upon her? What if Marian herself should give a glance of surprise at the old shabby gown? These were some of the troubled questions that whirled through Angela's head as she went down the stairs with Mary Marcy. And down behind them, following closely, though Angela did not know it, came the two Ryder girls, full of eager curiosity, for they were both of them now quite certain that Marian had received no note of any sort from Angela. "She didn't know enough to write an acceptance. How should she? I don't suppose she's ever had an invitation to a party in her life," whispered Nelly to her cousin in the first shock of surprise at seeing Angela in the dressing-room.

"No, of course not," whispered back Lizzy; and so, confident and secure in this belief, and in the anticipation of "fun," as they called the displeased astonishment they expected to see Marian express at the sight of her uninvited guest, and the guest's mortification thereat, the conspirators stepped softly along down the stairs and across the great hall into the beautiful brilliant parlor.

Marian was standing at the farther end of the parlor facing the doorway, with two of the Selwyn cousins beside her, as the fresh arrivals appeared. She was laughing joyously as they entered; but at her very first glimpse of the approaching group, the laugh ceased, and a look of sudden resolve flashed into her face,--a look that the Selwyn cousins, who had been told the whole story of the fraudulent invitation, understood at once to mean, "Here is my opportunity and I'll make the most of it!" But to the others--to the four who were approaching--this sudden change in their hostess's face was thus variously interpreted: "She has seen Angela," thought the Ryder girls, triumphantly. "She has seen the Ryder girls, and she is going to punish them," thought Mary, nervously. "She is looking at my dreadful old gown," thought Angela, miserably.

And moved thus differently by such different anticipations, the little group came down the room, Mary's nervousness increasing at every step,--for her shyness and the Quaker love of peace rose up within her at the sight of Marian's face, that seemed to her to betoken a plan of punishment for the approaching offenders more in accordance with the fiery Selwyn spirit than any spirit of peace.

Just what Mary feared she could not have told; but she knew something of this Selwyn spirit, and had often heard it said that the Selwyn tongue could cut like a lash when once started. That the Ryders deserved the sharpest cut of this lash she fully believed; but, "Oh, I *do* hope Marian won't say anything sharp *now*," she thought to herself. And it was then, just then, at that very moment, that she saw Marian's face change again, as the softest, sweetest, kindest of smiles beamed from lips and eyes, and the softest, sweetest, kindest of voices said,--

"How do you do, Mary? I'm very glad to see you,--you know my cousins, Bertie and Laura;" and in the next breath, "How do you do, Miss Jocelyn? It's very nice to see you here.--Bertie, Laura, this is my friend Angela Jocelyn, who is going to make one of our charade party next month if I can persuade her."

One of that May-day charade party! Mary opened her eyes very wide at this, and Angela wondered if she were awake. But the charming voice was now speaking to some one else,--was saying very politely without a touch of sharpness, but with a world of meaning to those who had the clew, and those only,--

"How do you do, Lizzy? How do you do, Nelly? And, Nelly, I want to thank you for a real service in connection with my birthday invitations. But for you I should have missed a very welcome guest. I shall never forget this, you may be sure."

"I--I--" But for once Nelly Ryder's ready speech failed her. Her cousin tried to take up her words, tried to say something about April fun, tried to smile, to laugh; but the laugh died upon her lips, and she was only too glad to move on with Nelly into the room beyond, and there, out of the range of observation for a moment, the two expressed their astonishment and dismay at Marian's knowledge, and wondered how she came by it.

"But to think of her taking an April joke so seriously as to make much of Angela Jocelyn just to come up with *me*!" burst out Nelly.

"And to think," burst out Lizzy, with a sly laugh, "that it is *you* who have introduced Angela to Marian's good graces, and that it is *you*, after all, who have been made the April fool, and not Angela!"

THE THANKSGIVING GUEST.
CHAPTER I.

"It is such a lovely idea, such a truly Christian idea, Mrs. Lambert. How did you ever happen to think of it?"

"Oh, *I* did not think of it; it wasn't *my* idea. Didn't you ever hear how it came about?"

"No; do tell me!"

"Well, my husband, you know, was always looking out for ways of doing good,--lending a helping hand,--and he used to talk with the children a great deal of such things. One day he came across a beautiful little story that he read to them. It was the story of a child who made the acquaintance of a poor, half-starved student and brought him home with her to share her Thanksgiving dinner. It made a deep impression on the children. They talked about it continually, and acted it out in their play. But they were in the habit of doing that with any fresh story that pleased them, so it was nothing new to us, and we hadn't a thought of their carrying it further. But the next week was Thanksgiving week; and when Thanksgiving Day came, what do you think those little things did,--for they were quite little things then,--what do you think they did but bring in just before dinner the half-blind old apple-pedler who had a stand on the corner of the street?

"They were so happy about it, and they thought we should be so happy too, that we couldn't say a word of discouragement in the way of advice then; but later, when we had given the old fellow his dinner, and he had gone, we had a talk with the dear little souls, when we tried to show them that it would be better to let us know when they wanted to invite any one to dinner or to tea,--that that was the way other girls and boys always did. They were rather crestfallen at our suggestions; for, with the keen, sensitive instinct of children, they felt that their beautiful plan, as they thought it, had somewhere failed, and, though they promised readily enough to consult us 'next time,' we could see that they were puzzled and depressed over all this *regulation*, when we had seemed to have nothing but admiring appreciation for the similar act of the child in the story. My husband, seeing this, was very much troubled to know just what to say or do; for he thought, as I did, that it might be a serious injury to them to say or do anything to chill or check their first independent attempt to lend a helping hand to others. Then all at once out of his perplexity came this idea of allowing the children from that time forward to have the privilege of inviting a guest of their own choosing every Thanksgiving Day, and that this guest should be some one who needed, in some way or other, home-cherishing and kindness. They should have the privilege of choosing, but they must tell us the one they had chosen, that we might send the invitation for them. This plan delighted them; and from this start, five years ago, the thing has gone on until it has grown into the present 'guest day,' where *each one* of the children may invite his or her particular guest. It has got to be a very pleasant thing now, though at first we had some queer times. But as the children grew older, they learned better how to regulate matters, and to make necessary discriminations, and a year ago we found we could trust them to invite their guests without any older supervision, and they are very proud of this liberty, and very happy in the whole thing; and such an education as it has been. You've no idea how they have learned to think of others, to look about them to find those who are in need not merely of food or clothing but of loving attention and kindness."

"Well, it is beautiful, Mrs. Lambert, and what a Thanksgiving ought to be,-- what it was in the old pilgrim days at Plymouth, when those who had more than others invited the less fortunate to share with them. It's beautiful, and I wish everybody who could afford it would go and do likewise."

"Speaking of affording it, I thought, when my husband died last spring, I should have to give up our guest day with most other things, for you know that railroad business that my husband entered into with his half-brother John nearly ruined him. I think the worry and fret of it killed him, anyway, and I told John so, and he has never forgiven me. But I have never forgiven him, and never shall; for if it hadn't been for John's representations, his continual urging, Charles would never have gone into the business. Oh, I shall always hold John responsible for his death, and I told him so."

"You told him so? How did he take that? What did he say?"

"Oh, you know John. He flew into a rage, and said he loved his brother as well as *I* did. As well as *I* did! Think of that; and that he had urged him into that business, thinking that it was for his benefit,--that no one could have foreseen what happened, and that if Charles lost, he also had lost, and much more heavily. But, as I was saying, I thought at first I should have to give up our guest day; but when matters came to be settled, I found there were other things I would rather economize on."

"Where *is* John now, Mrs. Lambert?"

"He is in--" But just at that moment a tall pretty girl of fourteen entered the room. It was Elsie, the eldest of the Lambert children.

"Why, Elsie, how you have grown!" cried Mrs. Mason, who hadn't seen Elsie for some months, "and you've quite lost the look of your mother."

"Yes, Elsie is getting to look like the Lamberts," remarked the mother.

"Everybody says I look just like Uncle John," spoke up Elsie.

"Oh, you were asking me where John was now," said Mrs. Lambert, turning to Mrs. Mason. "He is in New York, dabbling in railroads, as usual, and getting poorer and poorer by this obstinate folly, I heard last week. *We* don't see him, of course; for, as I told you, we don't forgive each other. Oh!" as her visitor cast a questioning glance toward Elsie, who had suddenly given a little start here, "Elsie knows all about it. Elsie is my big girl now. But what is it, my dear?--you came in to ask me something,--what is it?"

"It's about Tommy. He has told me who he is going to invite for next week,"--next week was Thanksgiving week,--"and I knew you would not like it, and I felt that I ought to tell you; it is that horrid Marchant boy."

"Like it,--I should think not! Why, what in the world has put Tommy up to that?"

"He says that Joe Marchant hasn't any home of his own this Thanksgiving, because his father has gone out West on business, and left Joe all alone with those people that his father and he boarded with just after his mother died; and Tommy pities Joe so, he says he is going to invite him here for next Thursday, and I knew you wouldn't want him."

"Of course not; the boy is ill-mannered and disagreeable, and he is always quarrelling with Tommy."

"I told Tommy that," laughed Elsie, "and he said he guessed he'd done *his* share of the quarrelling, and that, anyway, Joe Marchant was the under dog now, and he was going to forgive and forget."

"Dear little Tommy!" exclaimed Mrs. Lambert, admiringly.

"And he said, too, mother, that he knew you wouldn't object; that you always told him that Thanksgiving Day was the very day to make up with folks and be good to 'em, but I knew you *would* object to Joe Marchant, and so--"

"I--I don't know about it, Elsie. If Tommy feels like that, I--I don't believe it would be wise for me to check him. No, I don't believe I can. Tommy is nearer right than I am. He is doing a fine, generous thing, and it *is* the right thing, and I think we must put up with Joe Marchant, Elsie, after all."

"Oh, *I* don't mind, if *you* don't, mamma; but I thought you wouldn't like it, and it would spoil the day."

"No, nothing done in that spirit *could* spoil the day; and, Elsie, I hope the rest of you will make your choice of guests with as good reason as Tommy has."

Elsie looked at her mother with an odd, eager expression, as if she were about to speak. Then she suddenly lifted up her head with a little air of resolution, and starting forward hurriedly left the room.

Mrs. Lambert laughed as the door closed.

"I think I know what Elsie is going to do," she said smilingly to Mrs. Mason. "There is a young teacher in her school, Miss Matthews, who is seldom invited anywhere, she is so unpopular. I've often asked Elsie to bring her home, and she has always put it off; but I believe that this act of Tommy's and what I've said about it has made such an impression upon her that she has gone now to invite Miss Matthews to be her guest next week. She was going to tell me about it at first, then she thought better of it. They've all had this liberty for the last year--not to tell--it's so much more fun for them; and I can always trust Elsie to look out for things, she has such good sense with her good heart."

"Yes, and you *all* seem to have such good sense and such good hearts, Mrs. Lambert," said Mrs. Mason, as she rose to go; but as she walked down the street she said to herself, "Such good sense and such good hearts, overflowing with charity and forgiveness for everybody but John Lambert!"

CHAPTER II.

It was Thanksgiving Day, and just three minutes to the dinner-hour at the Lamberts', and all the guests had arrived except the one that Elsie had bidden.

"Don't fret, Elsie," whispered Mrs. Lambert to her, as she noted the two red spots burning in her cheeks and her anxious glances toward the clock,--"don't fret; she's probably going to be fashionably exact on the stroke of the hour."

Elsie gave a little start at this, and, laughing nervously, began to talk to Joe Marchant, while tick, tock, the clock beat out the time.

"We'll wait five minutes for her," thought Mrs. Lambert. "If there hasn't been an accident to detain her, she's very rude, and certainly not fit to be a teacher of *manners*, and I don't wonder she's unpopular with the girls."

The three minutes, the five minutes sped by, and the awaited guest did not appear. To wait longer would be unfair to the others, and Mrs. Lambert gave orders for the dinner to be served. It was seemingly a very cheerful little company that gathered about the dinner-table; but there was something pathetic in it, when one came to consider that each one of these guests was for the time at least sitting at the stranger's feast instead of with his own kith and kin on this family day. Mrs. Lambert herself felt this pathos, and it brought back, too, the losses and limitations in her home circle; for what with death and absence, her five children had no one now but herself to look to, where once were the dear grandparents, the fond father, and a score or more of other relations. But she must not dwell on these memories with all these guests to serve. She must put her own needs aside to see that little Miss Jenny Carver had a better choice of celery, that Molly Price and that big lonesome-looking Ingalls boy had another help to cranberry sauce, and Joe Marchant a fresh supply of turkey.

It was while she was attending to this latter duty, while she was laughing a little at Joe's clumsy apology for his appetite, and telling him jestingly that she hoped to see him eat enough for two, because one guest was missing,--while she was doing this, there came a great crunch of carriage wheels on the driveway, and a great ring at the door-bell, and, "There she is! there she is!" thinks Mrs. Lambert, with the added thought: "It's rather putting on airs, seems to me, to take a carriage when she is at such a little distance from us,--rather putting on airs, but--What *are* you jumping up for?" she calls out to Elsie, who has suddenly sprung from her seat. "What are you jumping up for? Ellen will attend Miss Matthews upstairs, and send her into us when she has removed her wraps. Sit down, Elsie; don't be so fidgety. I will--" But the dining-room door was here suddenly flung wide, and Mrs. Lambert saw coming toward her, not, oh, not Miss Matthews, but a tall gentleman with a thin, worn face crowned with snow-white hair; and, catching sight of this snowy crown, Mrs. Lambert did not recognize the face until she felt her hand clasped, and heard a low eager voice say,--

"I am so glad to come to you,--to see you and the children again, Caroline. I was away when Elsie's letter arrived; but as soon as I got into New York yesterday, I started off, and I am so glad to come, so glad to come;" and here Mrs. Lambert heard the eager voice falter, and saw the glisten of tears in the eyes that were regarding her and in the next instant felt them against her cheek as a tender kiss was pressed upon it. It was all in a moment, the strange surprise of look and word and tone and touch, the joyful cries of "It's Uncle John, it's Uncle John!" from some one of the children. Then all in a moment the strangeness seemed to have passed, and John Lambert was taking his place amongst them with the fond belief that he was his sister-in-law's chosen guest. And she, with those warm, manly words of thanks, those joyful cries of childish welcome in her ears, could she undeceive him,--could she say to him: "It was not I who sent for you; I am the same as ever, as full of wild regrets and bitter resentments"? Could she say this to him? How could she, how could she, when over the wild regrets and bitter resentments there kept rising and rising a flood of earlier memories of an earlier time when this guest had been a welcome guest indeed, and she had heard again and again those very words, "I'm so glad to come"? Those very words, but with what a difference of accent, and what a difference in the speaker himself,--only a year and his face so worn, his hair so white, she had not known him! He must have suffered,--yes, and she--she had suffered; but she had her children, and he had no one!

The dinner was over. They had all risen from the table, and were going into the parlor, and Uncle John had his namesake Johnny on one side of him and little Archie on the other. They had taken possession of him from the first, when Elsie, hanging back, clung to her mother and whispered agitatedly,--

"Oh, mamma, mamma, it was what you said last week about Tommy's invitation that made me think of--of inviting Uncle John; but perhaps I ought to have told you--have asked you."

"No, no, it is better as it is. Don't fret, dear, it--it is all right. But there is Ann bringing the coffee into the parlor. Go and light your little teakettle, Elsie, and make your uncle a cup of tea as you used to do; he can't drink coffee, you know."

The Codes Of Hammurabi And Moses
W. W. Davies

QTY

The discovery of the Hammurabi Code is one of the greatest achievements of archaeology, and is of paramount interest, not only to the student of the Bible, but also to all those interested in ancient history...

Religion   **ISBN:** *1-59462-338-4*   **Pages:132**
                                                   MSRP $12.95

The Theory of Moral Sentiments
Adam Smith

QTY

This work from 1749. contains original theories of conscience amd moral judgment and it is the foundation for systemof morals.

Philosophy   **ISBN:** *1-59462-777-0*   **Pages:536**
                                                   MSRP $19.95

Jessica's First Prayer
Hesba Stretton

QTY

In a screened and secluded corner of one of the many railway-bridges which span the streets of London there could be seen a few years ago, from five o'clock every morning until half past eight, a tidily set-out coffee-stall, consisting of a trestle and board, upon which stood two large tin cans, with a small fire of charcoal burning under each so as to keep the coffee boiling during the early hours of the morning when the work-people were thronging into the city on their way to their daily toil...

Childrens   **ISBN:** *1-59462-373-2*   **Pages:84**
                                                   MSRP $9.95

My Life and Work
Henry Ford

QTY

Henry Ford revolutionized the world with his implementation of mass production for the Model T automobile. Gain valuable business insight into his life and work with his own auto-biography... "We have only started on our development of our country we have not as yet, with all our talk of wonderful progress, done more than scratch the surface. The progress has been wonderful enough but..."

Biographies/   **ISBN:** *1-59462-198-5*   **Pages:300**
                                                    MSRP $21.95

The Art of Cross-Examination
Francis Wellman

QTY

I presume it is the experience of every author, after his first book is published upon an important subject, to be almost overwhelmed with a wealth of ideas and illustrations which could readily have been included in his book, and which to his own mind, at least, seem to make a second edition inevitable. Such certainly was the case with me; and when the first edition had reached its sixth impression in five months, I rejoiced to learn that it seemed to my publishers that the book had met with a sufficiently favorable reception to justify a second and considerably enlarged edition. ..

Pages:412

Reference   **ISBN: *1-59462-647-2***   *MSRP $19.95*

On the Duty of Civil Disobedience
Henry David Thoreau

QTY

Thoreau wrote his famous essay, On the Duty of Civil Disobedience, as a protest against an unjust but popular war and the immoral but popular institution of slave-owning. He did more than write—he declined to pay his taxes,   and was hauled off to gaol in consequence. Who can say how much this refusal of his hastened the end of the war and of slavery ?

Law   **ISBN: *1-59462-747-9***   **Pages:48**

MSRP $7.45

Dream Psychology Psychoanalysis for Beginners
Sigmund Freud

QTY

Sigmund Freud, born Sigismund Schlomo Freud (May 6, 1856 - September 23, 1939), was a Jewish-Austrian neurologist and psychiatrist who co-founded the psychoanalytic school of psychology. Freud is best known for his theories of the unconscious mind, especially involving the mechanism of repression; his redefinition of sexual desire as mobile and directed towards a wide variety of objects; and his therapeutic techniques, especially his understanding of transference in the therapeutic relationship and the presumed value of dreams as sources of insight into unconscious desires.

Pages:196

Psychology   **ISBN: *1-59462-905-6***   *MSRP $15.45*

The Miracle of Right Thought
Orison Swett Marden

QTY

Believe with all of your heart that you will do what you were made to do. When the mind has once formed the habit of holding cheerful, happy, prosperous pictures, it will not be easy to form the opposite habit. It does not matter how improbable or how far away this realization may see, or how dark the prospects may be, if we visualize them as best we can, as vividly as possible, hold tenaciously to them and vigorously struggle to attain them, they will gradually become actualized, realized in the life. But a desire, a longing without endeavor, a yearning abandoned or held indifferently will vanish without realization.

Pages:360

Self Help   **ISBN: *1-59462-644-8***   *MSRP $25.45*

QTY

The Rosicrucian Cosmo-Conception Mystic Christianity *by Max Heindel*   ISBN: *1-59462-188-8*   **$38.95**
The Rosicrucian Cosmo-conception is not dogmatic, neither does it appeal to any other authority than the reason of the student. It is; not controversial, but is: sent forth in the, hope that it may help to clear...   *New Age/Religion Pages 646*

Abandonment To Divine Providence *by Jean-Pierre de Caussade*   ISBN: *1-59462-228-0*   **$25.95**
"The Rev. Jean Pierre de Caussade was one of the most remarkable spiritual writers of the Society of Jesus in France in the 18th Century. His death took place at Toulouse in 1751. His works have gone through many editions and have been republished...   *Inspirational/Religion Pages 400*

Mental Chemistry *by Charles Haanel*   ISBN: *1-59462-192-6*   **$23.95**
Mental Chemistry allows the change of material conditions by combining and appropriately utilizing the power of the mind. Much like applied chemistry creates something new and unique out of careful combinations of chemicals the mastery of mental chemistry...   *New Age Pages 354*

The Letters of Robert Browning and Elizabeth Barret Barrett 1845-1846 vol II   ISBN: *1-59462-193-4*   **$35.95**
by Robert Browning and Elizabeth Barrett   *Biographies Pages 596*

Gleanings In Genesis (volume I) *by Arthur W. Pink*   ISBN: *1-59462-130-6*   **$27.45**
Appropriately has Genesis been termed "the seed plot of the Bible" for in it we have, in germ form, almost all of the great doctrines which are afterwards fully developed in the books of Scripture which follow...   *Religion/Inspirational Pages 420*

The Master Key *by L. W. de Laurence*   ISBN: *1-59462-001-6*   **$30.95**
In no branch of human knowledge has there been a more lively increase of the spirit of research during the past few years than in the study of Psychology, Concentration and Mental Discipline. The requests for authentic lessons in Thought Control, Mental Discipline and...   *New Age/Business Pages 422*

The Lesser Key Of Solomon Goetia *by L. W. de Laurence*   ISBN: *1-59462-092-X*   **$9.95**
This translation of the first book of the "Lernegton" which is now for the first time made accessible to students of Talismanic Magic was done, after careful collation and edition, from numerous Ancient Manuscripts in Hebrew, Latin, and French...   *New Age/Occult Pages 92*

Rubaiyat Of Omar Khayyam *by Edward Fitzgerald*   ISBN:*1-59462-332-5*   **$13.95**
Edward Fitzgerald, whom the world has already learned, in spite of his own efforts to remain within the shadow of anonymity, to look upon as one of the rarest poets of the century, was born at Bredfield, in Suffolk, on the 31st of March, 1809. He was the third son of John Purcell...   *Music Pages 172*

Ancient Law *by Henry Maine*   ISBN: *1-59462-128-4*   **$29.95**
The chief object of the following pages is to indicate some of the earliest ideas of mankind, as they are reflected in Ancient Law, and to point out the relation of those ideas to modern thought.   *Religion/History Pages 452*

Far-Away Stories *by William J. Locke*   ISBN: *1-59462-129-2*   **$19.45**
"Good wine needs no bush, but a collection of mixed vintages does. And this book is just such a collection. Some of the stories I do not want to remain buried for ever in the museum files of dead magazine-numbers an author's not unpardonable vanity..."   *Fiction Pages 272*

Life of David Crockett *by David Crockett*   ISBN: *1-59462-250-7*   **$27.45**
"Colonel David Crockett was one of the most remarkable men of the times in which he lived. Born in humble life, but gifted with a strong will, an indomitable courage, and unremitting perseverance...   *Biographies/New Age Pages 424*

Lip-Reading *by Edward Nitchie*   ISBN: *1-59462-206-X*   **$25.95**
Edward B. Nitchie, founder of the New York School for the Hard of Hearing, now the Nitchie School of Lip-Reading, Inc, wrote "LIP-READING Principles and Practice". The development and perfecting of this meritorious work on lip-reading was an undertaking...   *How-to Pages 400*

A Handbook of Suggestive Therapeutics, Applied Hypnotism, Psychic Science   ISBN: *1-59462-214-0*   **$24.95**
by Henry Munro   *Health/New Age/Health/Self-help Pages 376*

A Doll's House: and Two Other Plays *by Henrik Ibsen*   ISBN: *1-59462-112-8*   **$19.95**
Henrik Ibsen created this classic when in revolutionary 1848 Rome. Introducing some striking concepts in playwriting for the realist genre, this play has been studied the world over.   *Fiction/Classics/Plays 308*

The Light of Asia *by sir Edwin Arnold*   ISBN: *1-59462-204-3*   **$13.95**
In this poetic masterpiece, Edwin Arnold describes the life and teachings of Buddha. The man who was to become known as Buddha to the world was born as Prince Gautama of India but he rejected the worldly riches and abandoned the reigns of power when...   *Religion/History/Biographies Pages 170*

The Complete Works of Guy de Maupassant *by Guy de Maupassant*   ISBN: *1-59462-157-8*   **$16.95**
"For days and days, nights and nights, I had dreamed of that first kiss which was to consecrate our engagement, and I knew not on what spot I should put my lips..."   *Fiction/Classics Pages 240*

The Art of Cross-Examination *by Francis L. Wellman*   ISBN: *1-59462-309-0*   **$26.95**
Written by a renowned trial lawyer, Wellman imparts his experience and uses case studies to explain how to use psychology to extract desired information through questioning.   *How-to/Science/Reference Pages 408*

Answered or Unanswered? *by Louisa Vaughan*   ISBN: *1-59462-248-5*   **$10.95**
Miracles of Faith in China   *Religion Pages 112*

The Edinburgh Lectures on Mental Science (1909) *by Thomas*   ISBN: *1-59462-008-3*   **$11.95**
This book contains the substance of a course of lectures recently given by the writer in the Queen Street Hall, Edinburgh. Its purpose is to indicate the Natural Principles governing the relation between Mental Action and Material Conditions...   *New Age/Psychology Pages 148*

Ayesha *by H. Rider Haggard*   ISBN: *1-59462-301-5*   **$24.95**
Verily and indeed it is the unexpected that happens! Probably if there was one person upon the earth from whom the Editor of this, and of a certain previous history, did not expect to hear again...   *Classics Pages 380*

Ayala's Angel *by Anthony Trollope*   ISBN: *1-59462-352-X*   **$29.95**
The two girls were both pretty, but Lucy who was twenty-one who supposed to be simple and comparatively unattractive, whereas Ayala was credited, as her Bombwhat romantic name might show, with poetic charm and a taste for romance. Ayala when her father died was nineteen...   *Fiction Pages 484*

The American Commonwealth *by James Bryce*   ISBN: *1-59462-286-8*   **$34.45**
An interpretation of American democratic political theory. It examines political mechanics and society from the perspective of Scotsman James Bryce   *Politics Pages 572*

Stories of the Pilgrims *by Margaret P. Pumphrey*   ISBN: *1-59462-116-0*   **$17.95**
This book explores pilgrims religious oppression in England as well as their escape to Holland and eventual crossing to America on the Mayflower, and their early days in New England...   *History Pages 268*

QTY

The Fasting Cure *by Sinclair Upton*   ISBN: *1-59462-222-1*   **$13.95**
*In the Cosmopolitan Magazine for May, 1910, and in the Contemporary Review (London) for April, 1910, I published an article dealing with my experi-
ences in fasting. I have written a great many magazine articles, but never one which attracted so much attention... New Age/Self Help/Health Pages 164*

Hebrew Astrology *by Sepharial*   ISBN: *1-59462-308-2*   **$13.45**
*In these days of advanced thinking it is a matter of common observation that we have left many of the old landmarks behind and that we are now pressing
forward to greater heights and to a wider horizon than that which represented the mind-content of our progenitors...   Astrology Pages 144*

Thought Vibration or The Law of Attraction in the Thought World   ISBN: *1-59462-127-6*   **$12.95**

by William Walker Atkinson   *Psychology/Religion Pages 144*

Optimism *by Helen Keller*   ISBN: *1-59462-108-X*   **$15.95**
*Helen Keller was blind, deaf, and mute since 19 months old, yet famously learned how to overcome these handicaps, communicate with the world, and
spread her lectures promoting optimism. An inspiring read for everyone...   Biographies/Inspirational Pages 84*

Sara Crewe *by Frances Burnett*   ISBN: *1-59462-360-0*   **$9.45**
*In the first place, Miss Minchin lived in London. Her home was a large, dull, tall one, in a large, dull square, where all the houses were alike, and all the
sparrows were alike, and where all the door-knockers made the same heavy sound...   Childrens/Classic Pages 88*

The Autobiography of Benjamin Franklin *by Benjamin Franklin*   ISBN: *1-59462-135-7*   **$24.95**
*The Autobiography of Benjamin Franklin has probably been more extensively read than any other American historical work, and no other book of its kind
has had such ups and downs of fortune. Franklin lived for many years in England, where he was agent...   Biographies/History Pages 332*

Name	
Email	
Telephone	
Address	
City, State ZIP	

☐ **Credit Card**   ☐ **Check / Money Order**

Credit Card Number	
Expiration Date	
Signature	

Please Mail to: Book Jungle
PO Box 2226
Champaign, IL 61825
or Fax to: 630-214-0564

ORDERING INFORMATION

web*: www.bookjungle.com*
email*: sales@bookjungle.com*
fax*: 630-214-0564*
mail*: Book Jungle PO Box 2226 Champaign, IL 61825*
or PayPal *to sales@bookjungle.com*

Please contact us for bulk discounts

DIRECT-ORDER TERMS

**20% Discount if You Order
Two or More Books**
Free Domestic Shipping!
Accepted: Master Card, Visa,
Discover, American Express

www.ingramcontent.com/pod-product-compliance
Lightning Source LLC
Chambersburg PA
CBHW080909020726
47502CB00008B/2402